GW00750250

Behold Sarah

Lindy Henny

Clink
Street

London | New York

Published by Clink Street Publishing 2015

Copyright © Lindy Henny 2015

First edition.

The author asserts the moral right under the Copyright, Designs and Patents Act 1988 to be identified as the author of this work.

All rights reserved. No part of this publication may be reproduced, stored in a retrieval system or transmitted, in any form or by any means without the prior consent of the author, nor be otherwise circulated in any form of binding or cover other than that with which it is published and without a similar condition being imposed on the subsequent purchaser.

ISBN: 978-1-909477-95-7
Ebook: 978-1-909477-96-4

Before you start reading, I, Sally, Sarah Benson, want to make something clear.

If I kill myself during the time when I am writing this autobiography my story will stop before you get to the end, which is the moment of my birth. I am warning you because you may possibly feel cheated, not getting the full story. However, I am a curious and tenacious being. I do want to start living again and not continue this unbearable existing. I feel fairly confident that I will retrace my life's journey right back to the beginning, and in doing so hope to be enlightened, find a reason for my life.

A meaning.

Chapter One
Houseboat

'in the end is my beginning' T S Eliot

I live on a large, luxurious, beautiful, converted grain barge, sitting on the grey-green mud of the Thames – in Chelsea, of course – and I am sitting here too. I am also quite large and beautiful, and have, like my boat, converted often in the last sixty-nine years.

Now I'm in a bit of a quandary; that is to say I don't know whether to live or die. Have I now lived it? Has being human had enough of me, or have I got it wrong? What an unravelling has gone on, a winnowing and a threshing! I've wanted to unchaff myself right down to my essence, so little wonder my home is a grain barge, at the moment stuck in the mud and tethered to the bank. Me too.

When the tide comes in perhaps I should cut the mooring ropes and go with it, but the river flows both ways and that bit of driftwood that I am now watching can disappear upstream and come right back downstream to its starting point, here, just outside my window.

I like security, and that's why I'm here in Chelsea, with the watchman, the stout mooring ropes, and the gates marked PRIVATE (no hoi-polloi here!) I fit in well with the King's Road, its superficial eccentricity passing for originality. I am disgusted with my materialism, and yet I cling to it.

So I'm back to the predicament – it seems to me that the only way not to be what I don't want to be is dead. It's most annoying because I know I've almost made it. I'm nearly there, nearly a unique and wondrous being, but I'm tired and a mite confused. Perhaps I've gone as far as this human can. I am tired. I need to find God, I think.

GOD *quiscete et eum quaere i m speaking a little in latin as sarah loves it and it might help me to get through to her it gives me some gravitas she is studying latin in an evening class advanced level i remember when she was at school she did it for higher certificate she says she is confused from my point of view it is not confusing it is all so evident i really think i am evident dona dono dona in ludis facitis[1] sarah you do not think there is a donor or god there are signs abounding are you blind deaf obdurate stultissima[2]*

So the point of writing this is to seek clarification, and I hope I'll find the missing clues to what's fucking me up – stopping me living. I will, and I know it is going to take immense endeavour and resolve, recall events, people and circumstances throughout my life; significant happenings that hopefully may illuminate my purpose and meaning. Like Job, I rail at that God I cannot find.

GOD *adspicis in locum iniquum[3] do you hear me?*

'Did we come all this way for birth or death?' We'll see.

---

1 i give gifts you play games with the gifts

2 most stupid one

3 you do not look in the right place

I may sound pretentious quoting from *The Journey of the Magi*, but great poems are my gospels. This is a serious matter. The outcome of this research is suicide or life.

It is a glorious day, and I'm about to go to my club to play tennis. I'm apprehensive because I sometimes feel every bit of my sixty-nine years. For one thing, I'm not too fit at the moment, and for another I find some of the members there snobbish, and often bitchy.

I'm feeling chuffed because two weeks ago I decided to have some coaching.

My game is rusty. For heaven's sake, not surprising! I've only played about twenty times in the last forty-five years; when I was young I was quite a champion. The coach is older than I and an ex proper Champion. He is really toothsome, and most encouraging. I was absolutely relaxed as I felt I had nothing to lose, and although puffed and tired, after half an hour I'd gone through all the shots and he said, hear this, he said, 'Sally, your strokes are almost perfect, but watch the ball!' I felt like shouting with joy, and couldn't as I was out of breath. 'But,' he said, 'you must get fit. Start playing a lot, and then come back to me after I've finished at Wimbledon and Queens. Don't go to the other coaches while I am away. Give me your card and I'll phone you when I have a space.' How I wish I had been fit and slim, and somehow had amazed him.

I feel somewhat bad about you who are reading this because you may never know if I'm alive or dead, or doing the conventional thing of having an affair with the ski instructor – so to speak! But from my point of view it's on the cards. So I've been swimming a lot, when I can find time away from work.

I'm now putting on my newly bought sports bra, my

pleated skirt, my white T-shirt and am struggling inelegantly into my pants with a reinforced panel in the front.

Ready at last I pick up my racket and drive my bright red Micra to the club to find that club tennis has been cancelled because it is the day of The Garden Party. I am allergic to such events so fed up go home, reflecting on the way on how quite often I am motivated to do things because of men – like losing weight. I feel a bit ashamed that at my age I still behave like that.

I love sex. Ah, men! So be it.

It is a problem, isn't it? I long for something that I'm pretty sure I will not find, not now, and now is when I know how. Shit, oh shit, I miss him so! The near miss of a lifetime. Tears well up when I repeat his name. 'Samuel, Samuel, Sam, Sam.' A consummate soulmate, sexmate, playmate, workmate. Music, theatre, poetry, love-making, food. Then he died, not totally unexpectedly, but too soon, always too soon. I want to telephone him to talk about his death, and where's the reality in that? I want him to know that all along I knew he was a con-artist, an opportunist and thief, a womaniser, a phony, with a deluded sense of grandeur, and that I love him. I wasn't expecting a clue about my predicament so soon but here, I think, is one. Maybe I want to follow him. Not that I or Sam are sure, were sure, of a life after this, but there is an urge in a part of me to leave; my soul feels a magnet pull-away, and where's the reality in that?

I get out of my tennis gear and look at myself in the long mirror; the scars criss-crossing my stomach, my unfirm limbs, and feel bereft. Of youth, of vigour. Listless, I lie down on the sofa, propping myself up with a couple of kilim cushions behind my head so that I can watch the ducks and the geese on the river.

Why had I decided to live alone? John of the forty year

marriage is now living somewhere else; his departure left regrets and loneliness as well as relief. The latest attempt to be together didn't work out, so we split up yet again, with a financial arrangement meaning we no longer had the money that we'd had together, and this ex-poule de luxe is having to work much harder. I try to convince myself that what matters to me is integrity, not the money. What the hell! 'wotthehell wotthehell remonstrates mehitabel i cant work capital letters archy' I'm bewildered by the insistency of this driving force in me; the need to risk, to be true to my feelings, and myself.

But have I found myself, the one to be true to? And who cares if I am true or not?

GOD *deo gratia[4] sarah you do*

I'll answer my own question. I do.

GOD *you will not get anywhere like this i i i me me me you egocentric narcissistic in growing soul nail you block out those you want to listen you block me out too.*

I enjoy my work. The private therapy practice is booming. Lots of clients. I love it. It's such a privilege to be able to help people programmed by the past to free themselves so that they can discover and use the energy that was held back by indecision, fear, and habit. To watch them start to recognise, respect and express their feelings, and to find meaning in their lives. To help them come to understand and accept that pain is the manure from which to grow. I can wax lyrical about this work! As time passes, without any proselytising, each client becomes deeply interested

---

4 for god s sake

in their being, their soul, why they are here on this earth.

GOD *eheu sarah cur illuriem actis discebis*[5]

Not only those in this practice here in Chelsea, but also those inmates in London's high security prisons where for many years I worked with murderers, sex offenders, and men of violence.

GOD *i repeat why did you not learn from them?*

I have this feeling that I am passing through this human life, and have arrived at some level of consciousness that no longer needs this body.

GOD *a ha*

Yesterday evening Jan and Nicholas came around for our monthly Think Tank session. Our theme was Truth. Here is how it went, not word for word, but in essence. 'Truth is to be aspired to' 'Only aspired to, not ascertained?' 'Certainty is not possible.' 'We find truth in writing, sometimes.' 'Yes – through metaphor, parable, poetry.' 'Music, sometimes.' 'Art, sometimes.' 'It has to be out there. Objective.' 'Not between people?' 'Ay, there's the rub!' 'We humans!' 'Even between we three, can we be truthful?' 'Not from an absolute view point.' 'But we could try.' ' I trust you both, so can I be truthful?' 'You say that you trust us, but I wonder.' 'Right then, tell us how you truly are.' O the consternation in my heart. I hate him for asking that. I look so well, am beautifully situated in my boat, and now it's rocking near to sinking. I want them to... O fuck it,

---

5 alas sarah why did you not learn from them?

I'm dedicated to the TRUTH.

'I want to die.'

Silence.

'Histrionics!' 'It can't be true! You who have come so far!'

'What's this? You don't believe me. You, trusted friends, ha! cannot receive my truth?'

'But that's only part of your truth. There's a part of you that must want to live.'

'That's not the truth I'm talking of. The immediate bit that is now past wanted to die.'

'So you are telling us truth cannot be caught. It is ephemeral, only a vibration after it's been stated.'

'Yes, that was the truth but it isn't now.'

That finished that discussion.

Nicholas and Jan then asked whether I was fit to be a therapist.

I've often wondered.

'If you kill yourself, not you but your friends, clients, and children would suffer.'

Was I depressed? Should I have therapy?

Should not God-Life decide the time of my death? They missed the point. I am not depressed, just in a predicament. I feel played out. And if I am God-Life

GOD *optime[6] you're catching on*

I can create my own death. If it seems to happen to me, the 49 bus or something, in God-Life's timing, it is still me creating it. It is just a question of definition, and who is who, and what is what.

At this point I brought out some chilled white wine –

---

6 great!

Puligny Montrachet, of course!

GOD *benedicte*[7]

NB Something must be getting through, else how could I write down what I seem to hear? Strangely these thoughts or words type themselves out in italics almost of their own volition even though the font I use is Times New Roman. I am fascinated by the origin of words, hence my love of Latin. Clever and intriguing of someone to write it to me. Slightly doggerel though. If I managed to help my clients to find a meaning to their lives, by getting in touch with their feelings and freeing their thinking, maybe I should do the same . Free myself of taught thoughts and safe feelings . Break away from conformity.

---

7 cheers!

Chapter Two
Houseboat

As I have already mentioned I sometimes want to die; it seems too much to bear. Although it happened two years ago it feels too much to bear. Not only Samuel died, but also Gill, my sister. Gill a few months after Samuel so I will start with her.

Two things I have to hold on to. Firstly she had a quick and painless death. She blacked out, dropped down as she was hanging out washing on a cold December day, and although she regained consciousness for a short while in the ambulance Diana, her friend, told me she seemed scared; she died soon after, so she didn't suffer long, but I hate to imagine her being afraid and wish I had been with her. Secondly she would not like to have lived an invalid, and she wouldn't have done old age well at all, even a healthy one.

She had had a typical Gill week, rehearsing a Christmas entertainment in the village, buying presents for her children and grandchildren, cooking, doing the housework (she never had a cleaner as they were short of cash), walking her dog, Patch, on the common, and no doubt visiting 'Magic Land', a dell which she and I claimed as our own and where I planted an oak tree (Quercus) in her memory, and scattered her ashes; an oak tree is on our family crest.

As I write this I am crying, and saying to myself Gilly, Gilly, Gilly. After all this time! There seem to be no words to express bereavement, except perhaps poetry, but for me I use child language in a child's voice.Gilly, where are you? Come out, stop hiding! This is a silly game! Want to hug you, make toast in front of the fire. Then a shaking of my head, disbelief, bewilderment, and a great outpouring of love. Love you sweetheart. Thank you sweetheart. How well you could make cakes, and always a roast for Sunday lunch. How often we would laugh, giggle and cackle over mishaps and misdemeanours, often inappropriately. There was too long a time that I felt superior to you, so proud of my talents and achievements, and in my ignorant arrogance silently belittling yours.

I feel desolate but warm as toast toward you. I don't feel pain but deep deep sorrow, sometime spliced with guilt that I didn't tell you your worth. For many of our years together you knew how to love and give, and I only knew how to take. You were the witness of my life, always there and looking after me, Sal-belle, your little sister. I knew my past was real because you knew it. Feet-on-the-ground-Gill.

GOD *you are closer to her now than when she was alive*

It feels as if you have entered into me – I have become you and you me. I'm a little kinder now and simpler. Remember how insulted you were when I said I admired your simplicity. Like you I am worshipful of trees (I was better at their Latin names than you) and I shared your love, although not your knowledge, of birds. Here on the river I am surrounded by birds. They settle on the mooring posts, the cormorants drying their stretched out wings, looking like small German eagles.

I often think of your two rickety bird tables, and me

telling you off for spoiling the birds by continuing to feed them in the Summer. I miss the mint and the rhubarb from your small garden, and, and...

Each time I pass your photo on the chest of drawers in my cabin I touch your nose and say 'love you', and sometimes in my car I pat the seat beside me and say 'ride with me'.

GOD *and she does miraculum*

I remember, not in detail as it was a long time ago, before we were separated, how we had our mound in which we planted primroses, violets, daisies. And our war effort, a vegetable patch. Radishes and carrots, parsley and mint were our greatest success. We would go for long walks together, picked wild flowers and when we got back pressed them in between sheets of blotting paper, which was bright pink; I recall that vividly. We shared the book we put them in, carefully fixing them with Sellotape. In fact Gill took over because I just got gummed up; I still do, and have enormous difficulty wrapping Christmas presents. I was in charge of finding their Latin botanical names.

Earlier on, when in London before the war, we slept together at the top of the house. Our closeness and ability to talk about our feelings, and even at such a young age express our anger and sadness with Mummy and Daddy for what Gill called coldness, really helped us cope.

We did love them, very much, but understood that they had handed us over to be cared for by Nannies and Fraulein. We had Frauleins because Mummy came from a prominent German family, and wanted us to speak German, which we did – but forgot it after we left London. Her grandfather was the Kaiser's chest surgeon. I am not certain but I think they were Jewish because her parents came to live in England. Her father was married to an English woman. We never met them.

The last ten years Gill and I were close, and the very week she died we phoned twice, and on both occasions said we loved each other – normally we kept those sorts of feelings to ourselves.

We no longer believed in life after death as the church we once belonged to taught us, but now I think maybe I do.

GOD *a ha*

I often read *The Song of Solomon* – 'Love is strong as death and through our love you are alive.' I cannot credit my brain for understanding this, but some part of me does and that part knows there is no separation, that death does not touch the essence of our being, which seems to be linked to the vivacity of love, which knows no linear time.

NB So often I discount revelationary moments, discrediting them when I cannot determine their source. The bit above I've underlined I want to hold on to. It hints that Gill, It, and me are one. Does it indicate that I now believe in life after death?

GOD a ha

I notice that I have discarded that part of me that knows. I think it could be called my soul or consciousness. I need to recognise and reinstate my soul. Science has cast its spell over me for too long. I must take notice of italics when they appear. I miss those remarks in Latin however; miraculously; I did get Miraculum! And a couple of 'a ha's.

Chapter Three
The Flat on the Other
Side of the Park

Dead Samuel is here alive.

It started on a balmy summer evening and he and I were drinking whisky at each end of a bar in The Royal Albert Hall and were eyeing one another. I decided I wanted to know him and he decided he wanted me. So we moved to be beside each other.

'A Czech evening. I already know Dvorak, but am trying to expand my repertoire.'

'Smetana isn't so interesting, but Prokofiev is. Do you have a name?'

'Sally. Do you?'

'Samuel' – his voice, his voice – 'and I am another Czech here tonight.'

We talked until the bar was closed. We decided to meet at the cafe in the park near me next afternoon. Samuel stroked my bottom as we said goodbye. His knowledge and love of music, the whisky, the look and smell of him, the way he touched me. I was entranced.

So at three o'clock that Sunday afternoon we met in the insalubrious 'Park Awhile Cafe'. What a name, dear God!

DIEU *chacun a son gout*

We had a cup of tea and scones with strawberry jam and cream, the cafe transformed into a magical trysting place. We walked awhile and then went to his flat that was just on the other side of the park from my boat. We made love. Normally I would have said we fucked, we screwed, we had sex, that would be my language, but we were making love, the start of a great bond between us. I am unable to tell you how we were together physically, because I just can't write about the carnal side of things, but fucking became a paramount part of our love. It was the first time in my life that I had no reservations, no watching myself, or controlling myself or the man I was with; I had no fear, no fear of recoiling, pretending, of getting pregnant. I was in love, of love, by with and from love. And flowing.

I am going to try to tell you what being in love is.

All aspects of our lives were analogous. Samuel was, as I have already mentioned, my workmate, playmate, sex-mate, soulmate.

Workmate:

Sam was a writer – he had had a couple of novels published, one autobiographical about escaping the Germans, leaving Prague, the obscene murder of his family, and his coming to England after fighting in the French resistance. The other book was extremely funny and outrageous, in the genre of *Three Men In a Boat*. He also wrote for Jewish literary magazines. If he were still alive he would be reading this and helping me along; his command of English was superb. We loved to show our work in progress, benefitting from one another. He also wrote some poetry, but that was in Czech. Often we would lie on his soft leather sofa, me lying on top of him, my legs between his and my head resting on his shoulder and holding the book so we both could read it. I was introducing him to English poetry.

In our three years together we must have read most of my favourite poets, from Chaucer to the Beatles. We loved the sound of the words, and the sound of our voices. As he read I could feel the vibration of Dylan Thomas through the back of my head, and feel his breath on my cheek. Our senses were so enlivened that we often turned into each other, enraptured. The poem had no need to be a love poem to affect us, but once when we were reading e.e. cummings' 'now i love you and you love me' the last verse found us naked on the floor, 'we're wonderful one times one' – a line I said again loudly as I came.

As we were both word-smiths our poetry sessions were work and play.

Playmate:

We liked going to plays, films and concerts, or listening, often in bed, to music. One piece, Brahms' Double Concerto, would always entwine us – Sam said he often had used it to entice women into sex. Ecstatic music, ecstatic sex. Delicate Mozart trios, delicate sex. The physical and spiritual allied.

Sexmate. Soulmate:

I remember a student of mine telling me that she started to believe in God when having an orgasm.

GOD *one of my best invented sensations*

She felt herself in ecstasy, totally connected to something beyond the man she was with, full of love, receiving love, and something she could not define.

GOD *a ha*

I felt the same way when I came with Sam.

He and I shared what I called our WOW prayer. We would either say WOW out loud or say it silently – a moment of worship for an insight, a work of art, a great baked potato with loads of butter.

GOD *wows much appreciated*

Dear God, I am missing him.

GOD *dear sarah take him inside you*

We were so grateful for one another, and how we loved the smell and taste of us, our thoughts, perceptions, seriousness, talents, laughter, mingling, and silliness. Being in love is a composite of so many things. It is part soul, part mind, part body, and it gives glimpses of something I have not been able to name.

GOD singing *amo amas amat just call me love*

Aristotle got it right 'Love is a single soul in two bodies'.

Many of my poems are about love but this one is about Sam's untimely death.

GOD *it was timely.*

Or was it timely? You died instead of suffering.

I wait for you
boxed up with grief
a purple ribbon in my hair
break through my suffocating coffin
open me up
together we will breathe again

GOD *incorporate him*

NB What to say? I suppose I am beginning to realise the qualities I projected onto Sam were what I loved, although it seemed like the actual Sam to me. In reality he was an opportunist, a thief. Funnily enough I don't seem to mind that there is now no way that I will get back the £15 000 that I lent him to pay off some of his debts. He could have easily had a salaried job, but impressed upon me that he was born to be a writer, an author, although no new novel materialised. He said he would start paying towards our holidays and outings and pay off his debt to me when his next book got published. He omitted to inform me that he had a condition called antibiotic-resistance, which caused his death. Nor did he tell me that he had slept with a colleague and close friend of mine; at least not until I challenged him after I had found some girly pyjamas under his pillow. But he justified it saying it no way impinged on our sacrosanct love. He considered that he was a seer, had certain occult gifts and was a Christ figure not yet recognised as his time was still to be designated. He said all this in a sort of jokey modest way as if it could not possibly be true. But he believed it. It thrilled me when he sometimes called me Magdalene and enrolled me as his partner on his mission, his mission to awaken the world. Even now when I recognise his duplicity, and as a psychotherapist his grandiose delusional disorder, I still believe in him, magic and all! 'Sarah, he was not worthy of your love' 'Why did you go for such a charlatan – we saw it from the start' 'We warned you, Sal, but you didn't heed us' 'You'll be taking up with one of your prisoners next…' I loved him, am still in love with him. His flaws were part of him. Not worthy! What balls! He awakened me. By the way, just as with Gill, he is beginning to be part of me. 'And Death Shall Have

No Dominion', Dylan Thomas; one of our favourite poems.

GOD *i love in much the same way i am passionate about miscreants.*

Miscreants, miscreants, why am I thinking about miscreants? Ah, well! I have decided to tell you about the time I worked in a high security prison in London. And about that toxic industry. But before I do I need to inform you of some other chapters I am going to include.

When I planned to head each chapter of my story with the name of the place where I was living I limited myself, because quite a lot of my time throughout all those years was spent in a place that I will call 'My Hut' or maybe 'Willow Cabin' (and call upon my soul within the house). I could and still can fabricate the hut just like that (snap fingers) and it would erect itself wherever and whenever I needed it. I would go into my own private dwelling place and there would reflect, assess, question, learn to listen and eventually hear. So every now and then from now on you will see a chapter headed 'My Hut' or 'Willow Cabin'. I have not been able to put these chapters chronologically for in the hut time does not exist in that way, and what I thought then is now, and what I think now is then. Over the years the time spent in this sanctuary helped me become better at comprehending. I have learnt how to read between the lines, and am beginning to ask the right questions. In there structures melt, learnt rules no longer hold force, in fact new pristine thoughts and 'knows' arrive. With so much cleared out there is room for them, and in they come.

So here is my first 'My Hut' or 'Willow Cabin' chapter. I just cannot decide which heading to use so I'll use both.

Chapter Four
My Hut
Williow Cabin

Old age Death

I can't remember when I first came in here to think about death; my hunch is that it was at many different times throughout my life. I've always been intrigued by death, my mother's, the people who died in frozen positions whilst taking tea in Exeter after the blast from the bomb, suicide and its attraction. Just lately the deaths of Gill and Samuel. So this visit will be a collection of some of my thoughts and considerations.

As I am in my sixties I'm nearly there – I mean at the advent of my old age, which is the advent (a long one I hope) to my death; that is if I can get over this dispiriting feeling of just existing which tempts me towards taking my own life.

When does old age start? According to a national survey, at fifty-nine. I think, as do most of my friends, at about sixty-five. However, the when to me is of little importance, except I have the pleasure of applying for freebies – pensions, bus passes, TV licences. The only complaint I have is that I now get tired more quickly than before, and that, physically, like when playing tennis, I don't run for the ball, or a bus for that matter. Not that I ever did! Run for a bus, I mean.

The Cosmetic Racket is well honed into old age. All the stuff that most lucrative of industries (just after the arms and the pharmaceutical ones) bombards us with; how to avoid wrinkles, colour up your whitening hair, don't stoop, instructing us to walk tall as if your nipples are pointing straight ahead. Come to our Silver Workshops and exercise into Beauty, and at the same time buy our age defying divinely packaged products. Here is 'Flourish' to nourish your skin into a youthful glow. Anti-aging creams and lotions are some of the cosmetic industry's prime products. It treats old age as an enemy that must be conquered or at least camouflaged.

How about a Botox treatment, a chemical skin peel, a collagen lip plant?

I have just looked in the mirror that has suddenly placed itself on the cabin wall and had a good look. I like my wrinkly face, I like my sort of white hair. Funnily enough it is the colour that I paid a fortune for when I was in my twenties. Mr Teasy-Weasy convinced me that the time for orange, blue and bright green hair was over for me; I was to be beautiful, not zany! So sometimes I had the whole head done, but mostly he gave me platinum blond/white highlights. Not 'gave', it cost a lot of money, between five and ten pounds.

I must admit I am inclined to slump so will from now on point my nipples forward and ever forward.

I cannot be bothered to dwell upon my own old age but am aware that I want to help others come to grips with it – perhaps I'll run some workshops on the subject. When I do I'll have a mixed age group as I don't like categories.

Mirror, mirror on the wall… O, it has vanished. I've noticed poets put O not Oh.

I think it is a bad idea to classify people, for example 'the elderly'. Poor old thing, Sarah, limp into decrepitude, old girl! Having written that I am not concerning myself with my advancing years is not really true. I have been taken by surprise, they have crept up on me. One of the things I am anxious about is my sexuality – it does not seem to have diminished but it seems to be a taboo subject. It's as if it is unseemly for the old to desire, or, heaven forbid, make love. I remember I was told that after the menopause one dried up physically and didn't want 'it' any more. If the sexual juices are less active one can always use a lubricant.

'Sarah, you really shouldn't write about such things.'

All that menopause nonsense was no more true than the myth that elderly people do not feel sexy, want sex. Because the common attitude to the old being sexually active is so negative – I can almost feel the repulsed shudder – it seems to have affected many of my contemporaries. They are repressed, have repressed themselves as they do not want to offend. They have opted out. On the whole the elderly dress dowdily, unattractively. 'See how we have become!' 'You won't want to touch.' 'We are dried up and wrinkly.'

Where are the potential lovers?

So now Death.

The first death that nearly caused my death was my mother's. I was fifteen and had been separated from her for seven years. During that time I had only seen her once, when she visited Pinewood Lodge. All I remember was her coming into my bedroom one evening and saying, 'Sally-Sal, why did they take you from me?' I know I cried myself to sleep as I wanted to be with her, and in retrospect think it would have been better for me, even though she and my godfather, who was now her husband, both drank too much. Better to be loved by a drunk than live with coldness, and as sex fodder for an uncle. When she died, as you will read, I was so hurt I wanted and intended to die.

So here are two of my attitudes, my feelings about death. The loss of her, the thought of never seeing her again was too much to suffer, although in reality I wasn't seeing her, so it was the loss of the hope that one day I might be mothered and loved. It was not to be borne. Her death was terrifyingly final and cruel. For me not for her.

I hated death because of hers, yet at the same time loved it for me, as it was a way to end my anguish. Death I hate you. Death I love you.

It is obvious that I didn't kill myself as here I am typing away, but I have several times been tempted to permit suicide. Even in the first chapter of this, my story, I was thinking about it.

I have hesitated to put in words what I think about killing because many people will consider me beyond the pale. However, here goes! I see nothing wrong about committing suicide, except perhaps the pain and possible guilt it might inflict on those supposedly close to one.

I hate the legitimate murder in wars, and have been on many anti-war marches and taken part in innumerable protest meetings. Not that we had any influence on the course of events! It is not so much the destruction of lives that gets to me but war's inefficacy. Dialogue would be better, but loses out because of the corrupt arms industry, which makes money, money, money for so many people and governments.

I disapprove of capital punishment; it is hardly a punishment as death lets the perpetrator off the hook, and aren't the executioners murderers?

To kill someone is somehow a clean way to shut them up, get rid of them.

GOD *beyond the pale sarah*

I am not recommending it! But to me it is not the ultimate crime. Obviously the warmongers agree with me.

When working with murderers in prison I reached the conclusion that torturing someone by cruel, repressing, depriving or violent behaviour is a worse crime (though not registered as such) than killing someone. My prison governor told me that 70% of murderers were drunk or drugged, out of their minds when they killed. If they weren't addicted they would not kill, because they then would have been aware and afraid of the consequences and most likely would be unable to get into the predisposition needed to murder, to take someone's life.

The killing instinct is in each one of us. Maybe I'm wrong, but I certainly have it.

I was once so jealous that someone I was in love with was sleeping with someone other than me that I was ready to kill. The trouble was that I couldn't decide whether to kill him or her! The evening arrived when I was to do the deed. At the last minute and out of the blue,

GOD *if you want to call me that*

I decided to call in on a group of friends who I knew were dining together. I think I hoped they would dissuade me. They were people I loved and respected, including a high court judge, and a clergyman. I am sure I looked wild and dramatically magnificent! I told them my intention. They suggested that I give them the knife that I was sort of brandishing. Weapons they said are nearly always found and used in evidence, and told me of a much better instrument to use. I was to wrap a large stone in material

– a sock would do – and bash him or her on the head, then throw the stone into the Thames, go home and put the sock in the washing machine and turn it on immediately. They seemed to go along with me and my plan and were as helpful as could be. Then they offered me some wine, and then another glass and as far as I can remember another. I began to think of the sock I had to put immediately into the washing machine. Which one? A tartan one or the one with a Mickey Mouse motif? I began to laugh. So murder was averted. I joined them eating the dessert; it was peach flambé.

At that time causing death seemed to me no great problem, and the immorality of murder questionable.

GOD *think*

As I am writing this I find I have since then changed quite a lot in my thinking. Now I am disgusted by the murders, massacres and wars that are prolific, caused by rapacity, fear and that bloody arms industry. Random killing does concern me, but much more so the greed and unscrupulousness of much of mankind.

Abortion ranks as murder to me. Unless of course there are medical reasons for it.

Death itself is fine, says I, but the process of dying can be difficult.

Prolonged pain should be terminated by assisted suicide.

It is the human loss, the physical loss death causes that is hard to bear.

I have no idea if there is life after death. I'd like there to be. I sometimes think of all the work I have put into evolving, growing, understanding – not that it has got me as far as I would have liked it to. My effort must have been for some reason, and so I would like to continue after my death, at least my soul part, which I know I have but can't explain.

However, if I am just snuffed what would I care!

Death is a deadline, and as such acts as a motivator, a get on and do something with the time you've got left. Our space–time is finite.

GOD *so wake up sarah*

Something seems to remain after someone dies, not just memories but love.

Love seems immortal.

My thinking on killing is not consistent. First I say murder isn't immoral and almost condone it, then I am disgusted by it.

I imagine I'll be coming in here many more times to try to puzzle it out.

On the other hand I might just forget about it.

Concerning my own demise, I will go gentle into that good night.

Chapter Five
The Studio

just up the road

I don't think I have mentioned it, but I have been painting for the last ten years. It came about one day when I was very very cross. I can't remember what I was cross about. All I know is that I felt explosive. There was a canvas and some acrylic paint left from, I think it was, Richard's painting period. I squeezed out great dollops of paint, red, orange, purple, black and white, and with one brush after another scooped up the paint and thrust it on the canvas. I was swearing on each stroke and I have a rich swearing vocabulary. I covered the whole canvas and it was gloriously angry, the anger had left me and there it was in front of me. In a way it was an abstract painting, but there was definitely a snarl here, a punch there, and launched stones flying through the air. Having finished it I started laughing with a feeling of absurdity and great pleasure. So that started me off. Even John liked it, although his normal taste is pretty conventional. I had it framed and it hangs wherever I am living.

So for the last ten years I have had a studio just five minutes' walk from the boat, with wonderful light. There are three studios in this especially built block and we share a kitchen and a loo. I no longer paint with acrylic, I find it flat. But it made washing the brushes easy! Not so with oil. Oil is lovely to work with and I have found a quick drying oil paint. Patience is not one of my virtues.

The main reason I am bringing in The Studio is not because of painting, but because of my fellow artists. We are an unconventional lot. The three of them are younger than I, and more professional – making a living from their art. Two painters who share a studio, and one sculptor. I am only there one or two days a week, the others are full time. We always break at lunch time and sit together, eat, and talk. After it is dark we get together again and drink and talk. Our main subjects are creativity, our specific form of it, and what's it all about, the big IT. What matters and doesn't matter, and an insatiable curiosity about us as humans, and how we have limited ourselves. We all agree that creating a painting or a sculpture is the nearest we get to feeling we are God, or that God is working through us.

GOD *a constant worker*

Is there a God?

GOD *i know i am*

We couldn't be the original creator because everything we make is a copy. Even if it is an abstract painting (my style) all the colours and shapes had been picked up from somewhere.

I was particularly pleased to be with them because I could talk about some aspects of my life I had kept to myself. As they were interested and had experienced some similar happenings, and as they didn't think me mad or a liar I no longer mind talking, and now writing, about it.

I discovered just by chance I had healing powers. I will tell you about two occasions. This was the first time it occurred. I was upset for a friend; she was almost crippled with back ache. I asked her to show me the spot that hurt and she placed my hand on it. My hand started to tingle, and when I had stepped away my other hand tingled too. I didn't tell her what was going on and concentrated in directing that feeling of vibration toward her, specifically toward her lower back. It took about three minutes.

Then we had some tea, and shortly after I went home. It had all felt quite natural to me and I wasn't in the least alarmed, or even surprised. She phoned me that evening and said the pain had gone. She thought it might be some medication that she had been prescribed. I said how glad I was. I didn't tell her that I knew for certain how the healing had taken place.

Another occasion was when someone who knew her got in touch with me. She had a huge gland near her jaw that was affecting her ability to eat and impairing her speech. She was to go off to the States the next day on a talking tour and my bad-back friend had told her that she thought it was I who had cured her – evidently she had felt the heat from my hands. Could she come over? I didn't touch her but held my hands close to her face and directed the buzz from them toward the very large gland high up on her neck. I was strongly concentrated.

Before she left the next morning she phoned me to let me know she was catching the flight to New York, and the gland had vanished. I was happy for her, and not in the least bit impressed by what I had done. It all seemed so natural. Then I did get concerned as a gland came up just under my jaw and it was extremely painful. Physician heal yourself – and I couldn't. Something was wrong. I was taking the illness away, but I didn't get rid of it; it attached itself to me. Luckily I knew a well established healer. He healed me at long distance, and advised me that if I wished to continue I needed to work with a professional and learn not to take on the sickness I had freed.

Although at the time of the healings I felt at ease, and that what I was doing was natural, I started to think there was something supernatural about it,

GOD *mystical*

and it perturbed me.

GOD *beyond the natural world*

I decided not to carry on.
   I do wonder.
   Also I didn't want to take up another profession, therapy was more than enough. Somehow this form of healing was too 'magical' for me, and I felt it might take me to places I didn't want to go.

GOD *scaredy cat*

I needed to stay within safe limits. In the studio the four of us talked about using the gifts you have and that it was your duty to do so. I agreed, but still I dropped out. That energy, it seemed to me, could go any which way.
   I also told them that I once erased a talk I had on a tape. I didn't want John to hear it. It was about God and faith and I thought John might mock me. When he came into the room where I was listening and reached out to take

the recording machine I didn't touch it but said loudly in silence. No! The talk erased itself. The same energy?

Phil, the sculptor, had an out of the body experience when he had a crash on his motor bike, and when I was having a major operation I floated above myself and watched the whole thing. I could hear everything they were saying and was impressed how respectful they were, as well as how talented.

We talked about telepathy and knowing the future, and wondered why we didn't train ourselves in these abilities. I told them how I often knew more about my prisoners, even what crimes they had committed, than they told me. I remember an occasion when a murderer was talking about his victim, and without restraining myself I said 'what about the other one?' I was correct, and it caused quite a stir! Was he to confess to the authorities? Was I? A dilemma, because the group members knew there was a ruling that if anything criminal was disclosed it was to be reported. I wouldn't have done so, keeping to my therapy ruling – confidentiality. I was more than grateful that he, I thought courageously, went himself. His name was Al, a young man in his twenties, a recovering (I hope) heroin addict, unable to hold down a job and homeless. I think prison for him was the closest to being a home.

We four talked about the existence of God, meditation and prayer. And all sorts of things.

We agreed that we would help each other develop any of the gifts that we had – but haven't done so. Yet.

We are still at The Studio, except Geoff who got married and has moved to the country.

We have been lucky with our new girl, Serena. She is a watercolourist, talented and lovely.

GOD *you call it luck*

and I am lucky that I have my friends in The Studio.

GOD *luck*

NB I haven't noted the italic remarks. I wonder. Is what happens fortuitous? Since the deaths of Sam and Gill I haven't been going to The Studio. That's over a year. I had even thought of giving my studio up, but now that it has chosen to be written about, it has made me think. I recognise how important it is for me to be with people who want to evolve their way of living and being. I realise that that is what I want to do. There is so much more to being fully human.

Chapter Six
High Security Prison

GOD *reader you now know it is i speaking when you see italics so i will no longer put GOD anyway i don t much like having a name i am ineffable*

For five years I worked part time in two high security prisons in London. At that time there were no psychotherapists employed by HM prison service, only psychologists. My friend the Governor got me in by engaging me as 'Writer in Residence'. What an insalutary residence! I soon, particularly because he believed that therapy could benefit the inmates, was able to form groups of eight of them and usually had a therapist in training working alongside me, and often a probation officer – one of the few who showed interest in the efficacy of counselling.

I have always had a leaning toward the criminal, the miscreant. It felt like a vocation,

it was a vocation i vocated you

not that I would let that be known to anyone!

One day the Governor asked me if it would worry me to work on the wing where those committed for sexual crimes lived (I should have put existed not lived, or maybe rotted), separated from the other inmates for safety reasons. They were there for rape, repeated sexual offences, many against the under-aged, grievous bodily harm and murder. Of course I said yes. I had Mike, a student therapist working with me, and it was agreed that an officer be stationed nearby, but well out of the reach of hearing what we were discussing. The eight men had chosen to have counselling and Mike and I saw them individually to explain what the group was all about and to see if they were suitable.

It was to be six ninety minute sessions within three weeks, partly financed by a private donation and the rest by the prison service. Over the years over a hundred prisoners worked with us, but it became evident to me that the prison industry had no wish to see them rehabilitated – it needed the numbers, needed them to re-offend, so our work was sabotaged in many ways; for example the officers often didn't find the time to escort the men, 'we're short staffed, you know', and we would have to cancel, disrupting the continuity and depriving the project of many of its potential benefits.

There were some well motivated officers but too many of them were bullies, well paid thugs, pretty thick, with not an inkling about respect, except they expected it given to them because of their position. A number of them were appalling role models.

Sadly our short term interventions were of little lasting value to the men who worked with us, partly because the prison culture belittled and derided therapy and them for taking it. I have to admit I made a mistake, we should have done one to one work (we didn't have the money or the time) as it was impossible to get the men to disclose themselves in a group as they feared getting beaten up. It was considered weak not macho to be vulnerable; weakness needed to be hidden in such a predatory environment. There was a hateful pecking order of crimes and the pae-dophiles were considered the lowest of the low and were in real danger – the pecking could be lethal. I slowly began to realise that my aim to introduce therapy into prisons was being stymied. The psychology department wanted our money and felt their work was threatened by us, and so when my Governor went to Iraq to set up prisons , his substitute, a pal of the head psychologist, sacked us and the psychology department expanded. They didn't seem to be hands on, not dealing with the men's psychological and emotional problems, but observers who wrote up papers about the criminal mind! I felt my anger rising.

righteous anger

I was cross with myself that I didn't expose the prison system for the disgrace that it was. I was scared of reper-cussions. A colleague of mine had her car wheels slashed when she sort of whistle blew on some of the prison offi-cers' offences.

What a powerful intimidating union they have!

So much needs reforming; for example many a novice criminal would be banged up with hardened ones thus learning more tricks of the trade and most likely for good measure introduced to drugs. The drugs came in from all sources, in someone's hair, hidden in the body, passed while kissing, or thrown over the wall inside a tennis ball or perhaps a dead pigeon. I heard a prison officer say they often turned a blind eye as some drug taking made for a quieter scene. In fact drug dealing was a profitable source of income, and there were certainly screws (now I am slipping into demeaning prison-speak) who topped up their salaries by doing it.

There was a palpable feeling of malaise and boredom amongst the prisoners.

Men banged up sometimes for seventeen hours a day. My Nanny, if she had been there, would have tutted, 'Satan finds mischief for idle hands to do'. Apathy was creating angry young men, with no hope of sorting themselves out psychologically or bettering themselves. There was a minimum of education classes, and some other workshops such as carpentry, pottery and horticulture. Over 50% of the men couldn't write or read, or do basic arithmetic. Their brains were starved, and their bodies not well nourished. There was overcrowding and as meals were taken in cells, about 6 ft by 8 ft, one of them would have to sit on the lavatory and eat 'wholesome, nutritious, well prepared and served food' (prison rules dictate!). In truth it was bad chow, as they called it, over processed, stodgy, greasy with a lack of fresh fruit or vegetables. 'Pig-swill!' said one group member. I thought of Nanny again, 'Gill, Sarah, we are what we eat, so eat up your spinach, it is good for your brain'. The prison cooks peed in the sex offenders' food, many of the staff thinking that justified and amusing. However, in spite of some opposition we were able to set up our own kitchen with cooks from the unit. The meals were greatly improved, and those in our kitchen were learning a skill that could set them up when on the out.

There was not enough exercise or fresh air. Where were the creative activities?

Art, drama, communication skills – these had just been cut for financial reasons. No way for them to express themselves, no interactive therapy classes.

Maybe they would have a couple of talks from one of

the psychologists on anger management, but no help in understanding why they were angry in the first place. At least I understood why I became angry, endlessly ranting to myself – 'I am working in an ever an expanding, corrupt, pernicious, insalubrious industry'.

ranting is useful if it leads you to identify what needs doing
then do it

I considered most of the sex offenders mentally ill, and prison was not the place for them. Of course they needed to be shut away, but somewhere where they could have therapy, be understood, helped to change, and not despised and vilified. These were not bad men, but sick men who did bad things. They had with hardly an exception experienced the acts they had inflicted on their victims. Not murder, of course!

Mostly they were inarticulate, and could only deal with their low sense of worth with the help of drugs and alcohol. As I have already mentioned my Governor told me that most murders were done under the influence of drugs and drink. Shouldn't that be considered manslaughter, not murder?

The whole penal system needed overhaul. Most of these men would leave prison to face homelessness, unemployment and debt and the majority would be back here within a year.

enough reflection sarah do something about it

I decided that once I left I would get in touch with a prison reform society or start a foundation of my own. Here is a list of some of the changes that I felt needed to take place:

- different institutions for different crimes, with appropriate rehabilitation procedures. How about recovery wings? As about 60% of the prisoners' crimes are linked to alcohol or drug addictions, especial emphasis should be put on detoxification and treatment including psychosocial therapy. Less than 3% receive any help at all.
- different calibre of prison officer employed, after having a comprehensive training including a basic understanding of psychology and communication skills.
- a reforming, rehabilitating, restorative culture, with care taken of the language used both by the officers and the prisoners; how about calling them men or prisoners instead of inmates, cons, nonces or beasts, and staff instead of screws and pigs. In our sessions we called the prisoners by their first names giving them an identity and a sense of individuality, indicating our respect for them.
- a lively and appropriate education system so there is a possibility of employment on the out, including courses in cooking and nutrition so prison food would be naturally upgraded, and future work in catering a possibility.
- organised and challenging exercise, not just a stroll around the yard picking up the odd tennis ball!
- courses in communication – how to conduct oneself in a job interview.

How to deal with disclosure of criminal records.
- above all an atmosphere of respect, hope and positive intention for the rehabilitation and resettlement of the prisoners. I have repeated myself,

but will leave it like that as the attitude of prison employees is of immense importance.

I certainly couldn't respect many of the prison officers with their boorish ways and sick wit. Here is an example; when I asked them why they wore clip-on ties they quipped, 'don't want to be strangled do we now?' Perhaps I had lost it, but I found their jokes menacing not funny. I associated warders with shouting, swaggering, jingling large bunches of keys, slamming metal doors, and bad taste jokes usually at the prisoners' expense. They liked to think of themselves as dealing with dangerous men who needed holding down. They induced hostility.

I must say in all my time in prison I never felt threatened, or not befriended by the prisoners. They were courteous and would have been protective if need be. Only once did I ask to have someone removed from the group. I felt there was something wrong although I couldn't define it. However, I was right as I found out later that he had a history of hostage taking and maybe I was the next on his list!

Enough. I loved the prisoners I worked with and was enriched by knowing them. I left feeling sad, and impotent.

NB At the time I never did anything about it. I felt burnt out. A failure, and that those five years were wasted.

lived not wasted you learned a lot in prison you now have time on your hands

Now that I am retired, and am no longer in an all consuming relationship I have time on my hands. If I find the energy I might set up a foundation to start a private prison, or offer a service to run restoration and resettlement courses, appropriate education, and teaching skills to rein- stigate prisoners into society; in fact put some of the ideas I had into practice.

*nothing is wasted timing is all although time does not exist
    past present future are all one*

If recidivism is low as the result of the new methods we employ perhaps they will be introduced into state prisons. I thought those years were wasted, that I was on the wrong track

a wrong track can be a right track leading to a better track

but I learned a lot in prison, above all about redemption and not labelling. No-one is beyond getting onto a better track though it might take a lot of understanding, work and time.

there is a poem brewing

No Labels

*1. When dead
you can tag me
like the plan of the bull
on the butcher's wall.
That was her leg,
her shoulder, her brain.
But that's all.*

2. For now
do not label me.
Allow me
to move on
beyond the limits
of definition.
Once branded
I cannot escape.

Chapter Seven
Kensington Square

Each Wednesday morning about twenty-four of us aged between thirty-five and sixty years studied counselling techniques through discussion and role play. We were a mixed bunch in every way, differing in social and religious or non religious backgrounds, most of us pretty well educated, few with experience in psychology academically and others who had had some form of therapy, one to one or in groups.

Our jobs were varied. There was a young church army fellow working with alcoholics (I was bound to pick him out), a Buddhist professor of photography, an attractive self assured man, an Irish very funny nun, an evangelical preacher, an atheistic nurse, and an agnostic troubled and troubling woman who was preparing couples for their babies' birth. Teachers and social workers. All of us trying to improve the understanding of what we were already doing and aiming to become counsellors.

In the afternoon we divided into two groups with a different leader. That's the wrong title! Facilitator. It was called an experiential group and he, a very dishy Middle European man (I always seem to be attracted by non English men), nudged us skilfully into trusting each other enough to expose just a little of the soft, soft underbelly of our shelled existences. But no exposing of our genitals – sexuality was not touched upon. And not our souls. It seemed that therapy at this time didn't think we had them.

I, who looked so with it but was without it, found these thirty group sessions just what I needed. Risking again the feelings of loss and longing. Facing the fear of evil out there and maybe in me. To let the dreaming start again and the searching. What a relief to find the other group members similar to me and dealing with many of the same perplexities. I had thought them to be too pedestrian and grounded to have such problems and that I was a special case.

It was fascinating watching our small breakthroughs (the title of my collection of poems), witnessing the shift of an expression, the shaved off beard, the pair of bright coloured shoes that walked in one day on the most unlikely pair of legs.

So much change.

So I became a person who sits once a week in a room off the King's Road, waiting to see if anyone feels like talking to me. It is a friendly room, fresh and attractively decorated with comfy chairs and tables to lean on, put our mugs of coffee/tea on. We get it from a bar womanned by Elsie and her friends who make most excellent snacks and sandwiches (which I get free in lieu of payment). The cost is minimal or nothing if someone is really out of funds. Elsie and her helpers are the most experienced informal counsellors, untrained except by life, intuitive and droll as is the Cockney's heritage, inspiring confidence and keeping it, and not missing a trick. I felt the probationer!

My first time there, waiting for a client. I feel apprehensive. O Ear that is sticking out and listening (I put that in as our service was called The Listening Ear) and the inevitable cup of cooling coffee/tea lasting itself longer – the one common denominator between me and the man sitting opposite. Will he talk to me? My first encounter. I'm sort of reading *The Independent* and he is carefully reading I'm not sure what. I chose my paper on the way here as a possible starting talking point; not too up and not too down, like the jeans and pullover I am wearing, and natural coloured nail varnish, having removed the crimson one this morning. To be yourself or not to be?

He's large, about fifty, should be jolly but looks agloomed. Between us are our cups, the brown liquid ominously descending, and us pretending to read our papers, his of little format making mine look aggressive.

I read.

I sip.

Then say, 'First time (lie) I've read *The Independent* – quite hard finding your way around a new paper – have you tried this one?'

'No – I think *The Guardian* good.' (Mental note: I'm sure he has never read it.)

'Because it's sort of in the middle.'

'Yes, not too right and not too left.'

'Kind of reasonable.'

'Yes.'

'Yes.'

'Yes.'

'With a name like *Independent* it should be too. Nice name *Independent*.'

listen sarah keep quiet

Sip.

Sip.

just wait

Chair scrape.

'I really should go back…'

We actually look at one another. I notice that his chair has moved in towards our table as if he is staying put.

'But you know how it is.' The gentle Irish voice, quiet, restrained, coming from this great florid looking man.

Sip.

'I'll be going to the doctor for the state I'm in.'

'Mmmmm' in my best counselling indoctrinated fashion. Imagine my dead father or my stoic husband, not half as manly looking as the man opposite me, admitting to nerves.

'May go this evening after I've finished work, so that I'll get a certificate to take time off away from him – and maybe I can be off for good if the doctor tells me what a state of nerves I'm in.'

'Where is your work?'

'In the university over there – it's a terrible place to be.'

'I thought it might be rather cultivated.'

'Cultivated, my arse. A jungle a real jungle.'

'A jungle.' (Repeat last word when stuck.)

'A jungle because of him…'

'Him?'

'And her.'

'Him and her.' (I see pink and blue dainty towels upon a rail.)

'He's in charge of us and she of them. Two of a kind in charge of personnel. He has it in for me. Wants me in a place down there (thumb down) and keep me there. It happened last Wednesday and it got back to him. I was carrying two large plastic sacks of rubbish, helping the cleaner out, heavy they were to be sure, and this engineer type, a visitor, he asks me how to get there or somewhere, and I tell him, and he asks again and then I explain again about the lift and he, the engineer, he asks again. The bags are heavy and I put them down and he reports to him that I had shrugged him off, and I am brought up short and told to go home – put a bit more crudely than that.'

'How awful you must have felt.'

'Mmmm – humiliated.'

'And angry.'

'Angry. Very angry, I would have liked to hit him. There is nothing that I can do about it. But it has got to me. It keeps happening. I have this uniform you see, with braid, good buttons, smart shirt and shoes. I am on the main door entrance. I've another fifteen years to go before I get my pension. I shouldn't leave. He saw me yesterday and said "you're OK?" "OK," I said.'

'"OK" you said. You aren't. You are hurt and furious.'

'He mustn't know, he'd think I'm not a man. I liked my job, would do extra hours without being paid because I wanted to and now he makes me work overtime and doesn't give me a penny. I'm getting paranoid. It must be bad of me to be bending your ear like this. I went out and got drunk last night.'

'How's the hang-over?'

'None. I take this marvellous stuff you know, that grabs everything on the inside of you and sort of absorbs it away. You see this (indicating and rubbing his fairly ample stomach), it just remains the same. It just takes the fat away. I'll give you the name of it, you might find it useful. I must be going back, get changed. I hope I'll not be bumping into him.'

He pushes his chair back mournfully, picks up his mug despondently and heaves himself up in to an almost upright position.

'And if you bump into him (it's not your job to give advice) you make a sign like this.'

I make a vigorous V up towards the ceiling. 'That from me to him for you.'

Up straight he stood and grinned. 'And you with your posh accent! I'll give him a sign like this.' With his middle finger he impaled his enemy an d laughed.

'From me to him. Maybe I'll be seeing you again.'

With a jaunty bow he left.

O God, I thought, you broke at least one of those clear cut rules of counselling.

Don't give advice. He'll get the sack then die of nerves, or murder him.

That was my first effort of the day and the first informal therapy session I did after qualifying. There was one more person at another table whom I thought to be a potential customer. I moved over to her and enquired if I could sit with her.

After talking and drinking more coffee/tea, I thought she was in a rather poor off way – neurotically I mean – and discovered through careful listening that she was another newly qualified therapist like me!

The next week the Irishman was there again chatting animatedly with two men.

He seemed OK. He didn't appear to notice me, but as he was leaving I had to know.

'How's work?'

'Just fine. He's still a bastard, no changing him, so I'll be looking for a better job.'

'And when you bumped into him?'

'I ignored him. He's just not a man. I must be getting back. Would you be a single lady, or not?'

'Not.'

'By the way my name is Patrick, and yours?'

'Sarah.'

'Maybe I will be seeing you again.'

I must say I felt good. I really believe if I can be myself and find what tickles someone into changing, in Patrick's case from passivity and defeat into being in charge, I might one day make a counsellor.

NB Looking back at the notes I wrote after that day I realise how important that informal session was. Patrick was falling apart when we started talking, feeling powerless, unable to confront Him, accepting the role of victim. My notes mentioned how I made him laugh with my V sign gesture, and that he found energy in making his more crude 'up yours.' He felt witnessed by me, and understood. He felt he was a man, and Him wasn't. His self respect was restored and he was in charge of his life.

I picked up from that meeting the therapeutic value of being real, being supportive, manifesting to Patrick that he mattered to me, and that it is important to talk in everyday language. I try to keep the feeling of informality in all my therapy sessions and create a relationship that is trusting, expressive and loving. Agape, not Eros!

Chapter Eight
My Hut
Willow Cabin

Sex

This visit must have been when I was in my late forties.
Once I had sorted out my sexual hang-ups.

I took a puzzlement in with me, sex... I bemoan the fact
that the so called love affairs both John's and mine caused
us to separate at that time mine was with Michael and I
have forgotten about it except it broke us up John and me
it seemed that it was proof of the end of our marriage sad
very sad unfaithfulness adultery both recognised as justi-
fication for divorce wrong the whole sex thing has grown
out of proportion pulsating penises

I can even say the word now what a hullaballoo there
is about it used to sell almost everything even cars berum
berum are called sexy it spices up television the news
advertising literature why because of the myths it is the
ultimate experience a little daring naughty dangerous a
sign of how desirable wonderful it and you are above all
indicating that you o you two are meant for one another
made in heaven it is such an all important part of life
society's censure of free sex is a leftover from the time
when there was little or no birth control except premature

withdrawal spoiling the climax and often the carpet or the sheets then not so long ago the possibility and fear of unwanted pregnancy was real sex had to remain within the marriage so that if children resulted they would be looked after provided for surely contraception alters this

I am coming to the conclusion that sex should be let off the hook let loose let to be like an extended handshake an accepted form of communicating relating joy in life as god did I say god wrote in italics an orgasm is one of his best inventions why his why not her her invention neither god is sexless what a relief however there are certain cave-ats come to think of it which is what I am supposed to be doing in here these thoughts are only my opinion I guess not many people will agree with them and do I care back to the caveats FIRST no one should be hurt or deceived if sexual intercourse was not considered such a momen-tous thing was recognised as lust not love sex is not the currency of love that might help to get it into perspective

SECOND sex affairs should be discreet regardless of rationality your love partner will be sad at the loss of sex between you possibly feel jealous or envious of your new sex partner possibly possessively hate the thought that you are intimate with someone else possibly ay there s the rub in more than one way o witty why can't we be intimate with more than one person why are we possessive how can we possess anyone

I'm not getting this issue sorted out is it possible that we are created to be monogamous monogamous sexually don't think so we are created is there a creator if so if so how the hell are we meant to know what is expected of us digression to resume THIRD no baby should be con-ceived unless the couple are in a position to have a family however I am more than glad that there were three babies for us to adopt

I wonder how they are and what their attitudes to sex or anything must get in touch why is it such a taboo subject even liberated me am I get thought bound unable to write talk about the sex act it is too personal too private too don't know I do not want to think about it maybe it is more than carnal contraception in the soi disant developed world is easy now why make a moral issue out of it sort of do after all it is only sex sex is not love it is an instinct I am confused so what's new pussy cat it is possible to make love love love certainly definitely wonderfully more often it is just having sex intercoursescrewingcopulatingshagging-fucking one thing that might help sort matters out is to do some renaming sex affairs not love affairs sex partners instead of lovers rename my lover my squeeeeeze my flame corny unromantic not that I have one at the moment my thoughts are going each which way exhausting…

I am now lying on the really comfortable bed in my hut and I am thinking about a conversation I had. …it was at the party we gave after Caroline and Nigel's marriage it was a church wedding with all the trimmings a very happy occasion a long o dear time since I last saw them put this idea about freeing sex to a middle aged tousle haired man an international lawyer he turned out to be told me he had four sons two of them were at the wedding I guessed he was from a conventional upper middle class background like I suppose I am too he and I liberated love making fucking sexual intercourse whatever you like to call it we allowed extra marital affairs after all straying spouses were only having sex and getting close to someone other than their so called legitimate partner we divined that if it was not considered an act of unfaithfulness and a criticism of a marriage more couples would not break up he and I both agreed that after time the sexual urge and enjoyment diminishes between most couples we actually thought between all couples though you hear rumours I said I guessed the run down happens after about ten years he thought after less about seven these statements made us laugh as we were revealing that we both had had out of marriage affairs often after sex has slunk out of the marriage the desire is just waiting there until it finds another mate somebody new it need not demand you to replace your partner nor diminish the love within your marriage sexual need a physical want is being satisfied not unlike the pleasure of eating after hunger must get to Sainsbury we are out of salt dishwasher liquid as well as food should write a shopping list it's maddening I have no mental discipline off I go with almost worn out plastic bags praising myself for helping with the war effort what a flashback doing my bit to save the planet rubbish helps not at all unfaithfulness to love caring nurturing a very different matter that really matters we were totally d'accord shook hands and kissed…

I imagine he is in a great marriage and happily having sex affairs I sometimes feel a bit past it too much effort time consuming after our meeting I was turned on again he and I could have under different circumstances made love had sex fortuitous meeting affirmation it was good to get sex in perspective especially after the exhortation in church in the name of God forsake all others keep thee only unto her him him him her her some thinking and hearing what that God thinks now might not be amiss then maybe some revising of the vows after all God invented contraception

I left the hut quite pleased with myself feeling sexy and at one with my attitude.

As I was closing the door I am thinking I don't think my thinking has got it quite right. If John and I had thought about sex as I do now we wouldn't have needed to separate. By writing this, things are sorting out, clarifying. I am thinking quite a lot about John.

Chapter Nine
Consulting Room
Hammersmith

His name was Erik. He had studied with Grodeck, had a little white beard, and two dachshunds who slept at his feet. He had a gentle voice, a sense of reality and humour. The first year I went to him twice a week.

It is hard to tell how this analysis worked, or how it made me healthy in the long run. I started by talking about what happened to me whilst staying on the island, with the children and John. It was our fifth summer holiday there when I broke.

How confusing was the beauty and horror of it all – beautiful children, husband, the place, and how fearful and near suicidal I felt. My self-constructed self was falling apart. And then at home in London, there was the incident of the perceived sexual threat the evening before my legs became paralysed.

Of course the version I am giving you of our verbal exploration into my psychological dilemmas is not nearly as meandering and abstruse as it really was. How Erik helped me clarify and reach reality was remarkable.

Having set the scene I decided to proceed with two aspects of my life that were in disarray, although there were many others. First, me trying to be a mother, and second my inability to enjoy a sexual relationship, or even just a relationship with a man.

I told Erik how terrified I was that I might let myself leave my children, either walk away, or maybe kill myself to stop the anguish of being such a failure. Of course he picked up the phrase 'walk away' and connected it to my paralysis. I was encouraged to talk about my mother, and found I stammered on the M. M m m...mother M m... mummy. I didn't understand the relevance of that, except that it was a sensitive subject that at some level I didn't want disclosed – my secret. Until I talked to Erik about her I didn't realise or know how much I loved her, and at the same time hated her for abandoning me. Through my imagination I had built up the image of a caring mother, with me as her love and first concern but in reality she frightened me – the drinking, the physical contact, the fear of the hot milk spilling on me when she made cocoa on the gas burner in our bedroom, the desperate feeling that I had when she was crying and unsteady. Yet I loved her, my time with her, our performances for the wounded troops, our knitting (what a mess!) of wrist warmers and balaclavas to be sent to the front. We laughed a lot. And then I was removed from her without any explanation. I knew she was to blame, and that it was only partly to do with the drinking. She wanted to go up to Scotland to be with her lover, my godfather, rather than be with me. I had read some love letters that she kept in the drawer where I found the whisky bottles. From the moment I got into that police car I managed to feel nothing. She had left me to the wolves. I was brave, loyally loving to her, and showed the world that I could cope. I never cried, but had regular bilious attacks instead, getting rid of all I couldn't digest – at least that was Erik's interpretation. With my ability to repress feelings they had to get out somehow!

Maybe subconsciously I was put off being a natural mother because of her.

I hadn't had my own children although there was physically nothing wrong with me. Had I killed the sperm or the ovary in my own body through something stronger than conscious thought? Something stronger than the contraceptive devices I once used. Was I frightened to become like my mother, and repeat her rejection of Gill and me by abandoning my children? Had I thought at some level that adopted children would be safe from my sick inheritance? Was there something bad in my blood?

I never lay on Erik's couch as it made me feel too vulnerable. I sat in an upright chair looking straight at him, keeping a watchful eye. However by the end of the therapy I didn't need to keep on the alert. I trusted him.

Perhaps this poem that I wrote at the time partly describes the therapeutic process I was going through. I suffered as much pain as I could bear. I wanted to kill someone, or myself. I moved from violent thoughts and intentions to enfeeblement and passivity; eventually to clarity and moderation.

Antidote The Murderess and the Healer

As from the viper's fangs
the venom dripped from me.
Yellow droplets milked from the past
by gentle hands.
The poison lies there
an amber pool.
Foul.

We will distil it.

Take drink these limpid drops.

I'll not kill.

The way I thought about the paralysis, which was from the waist down, was that my unconscious had cleverly found a way to stop me having sex. Erik and I had two different interpretations; as I mentioned he thought it was to stop me walking out on my family – but maybe both explanations were correct.

We now looked at my fear of sex, and my distaste for most men. Over many months the disowned memories of sexual events in my childhood surfaced.

I'll just list some of them here. The headmistress caning me and 'favouring me'.

My great uncle having sex with the scouts which Gill and I partially witnessed.

Uncle David coming into my room at night, using me on and off for three years. I recalled a time when I was about fifteen at The Grand Hotel in Folkestone, dancing, held too close by my father who was often slightly drunk and overtly amorous, and my horror at his sexual arousement – my stepmother was there too, also inebriated, relishing the scene. The alcoholic drives home were horrific. There were pornographic and sex magazines in the car – I tried not to look at them, but my curiosity got the worse of me. I was shocked and yet intrigued.

Saturday nights were dinner and dancing and when I was there during part of the school holidays we would go out as a threesome – one of the problems was that they drank too much, and God knows why we didn't have an accident.

i drive well and took the wheel

Later, when I was about twenty I had a wish to be a prostitute, a fantasy that I really enjoyed. I actually befriended Yvonne who worked in Carlos Place but she dissuaded me saying I was too fragile. Me fragile! I had thought I was courageous and tough, a tough cookie, and well suited. I was totally confused. Sexual intercourse, which I knew could and should be wonderful, was ruined by looks that seemed lecherous to me, by touching that was repugnant to me, and potent sexual smells. I have to admit Yvonne was right, prostitution was not for someone like me.

There was another character that I liked to think myself to be. I thought I was a superior being with potent powers – extraordinarily close to being a magician, or Christ. Someone who could walk on water if she felt like it. Certainly I believed I could control or create events. We got that sorted by Erik inviting a healer cum psychiatrist to a session. I was hypnotised and in that two hour session, through question and answer, storytelling and conversing at a very free level, I moved from believing myself extraordinary to being able to say, and with great relief, that I was ordinary. I had joined the human race. I could deal or learn to deal with events as ordinary Sarah. To be honest I can't remember those two hours clearly. I know I had an injection, pentothal the truth serum, and all seemed like a dream world. It was an ordinary me who went home that evening.

There was a great deal of work to be done as you can imagine, and we did it. I had created a Sarah that was to the world a great wife, mother, home maker, confident, attractive, seductive – doing interesting work teaching part time. I had to permit myself to break down, deconstruct and transform. Face the ghosts and lay them to eternal rest.

It took three years and a lot of money, but what a release. Erik accepted me, talked with me, was in touch with my suffering. He understood me, and helped me understand myself. He helped me trust.

The truth does set you free.

NB It was such a success that I was determined to train to be a psychotherapist. I registered to do a four year training both as a group therapist and one to one. It fitted in well with my home life as it was only one day a week in term time with the occasional weekend seminar. It cost a lot of money but luckily John had a good salary and although he wasn't pro things psychological encouraged me to go ahead.

After I had finished my sessions with Erik I was able to see how working through those ugly happenings had increased my understanding of human nature and myself. Having looked at what I wrote about in the chapter 'Consulting Room' I can say that even if I had some difficult and endangering times when I was young they had been helpful and edifying in the long run. Those italics about taking the wheel. I had nearly written down that it seemed I was in safe hands.

Thank God (a ha!) for Erik and good psychotherapy.

Chapter Ten
The Apartment

on an island in the Mediterranean

FOR SALE

Ideally placed
pieds dans l'eau
view over harbour
sound of the sea
cicadas and gulls
scent of rosemary
easy access
to each other
sailing swimming
inland walks
coves for picnics
fig trees fishes wine
perfect environment
for growing children
sun guaranteed

SOLD

'What a good investment, the children will benefit from

these holidays for life.'

Here it was, your holiday home. Five years of island beauty, fresh blown air. Young lives muscle-building in the sea, against the strain of sails and waves. Skin browned to show the bright of teeth and eyes. Lifetime friendships forged with the elements, and short term friendships played with boys and girls. Walks into the pine woods, into the heather, rocky hills. Intimate picnics on sandy towels. Unoiled cicadas whose incessant sound beat murmurs of revelation. Salt whiting water and water washing salt away, and sleep like rest to start again reality. Your hair, hair-brushed sometimes by the wind. Your apples eaten and your laughter yours. The grass your mattress and the rocking boat your bed at sea. All good. You well formed and shining, the sun on your side, the flow of your lives free and forceful.

Out of the reach of my death.

I was full of fear. The apartment and the isle sought my death. 'I hope the children cannot notice that I hate this beautiful place.'

The gulls are laughing and the wind blows cold. Somehow the time I was in Devon as a child resurfaced and this is what I wrote.

It is with great fear that I disclose the nature of my sojourn there
a trembling angry jealous ghost dark tentacled with hate
pulled down to the pith of pain
to where the forces were so strong they could have reached
from this world to the next
Laughter bubbling from a source open to tears
a body young and fashioned by the waves
tough and anticipatory
pushing to be touched and mingled

to caress a sunlit body
spread out in acceptance of the moment
to stride long towards a fervent life
rich blood pulsing in such a rhythm
that made each entry exit climb surrender
each seeing joining feeding sleep a celebration

Her thoughts sang with the tides
felt fish were cider apples
the green grass shoots grew hay through her
made pillows for her head
juices spilt from her
she was creation's love-child gold and strong

A cold wind brushed her
limbs laboured and her blood was thinned
she withdrew to the shadowed land
of desertion and despair
and stayed there betrothed to death

I know that is not great poetry and a bit disarrayed but the poem searched me out; it wrote itself, and that interests me. There is a part of me trying to get heard. I may need some help.

'My love we're leaving, the children and we are safe.'

John decided that we should cut short our holiday, only by a few days, saying something – I forget what; a believable reason why we should leave, not mentioning my emotional state. I didn't feel unhinged or mad, but threatened. The contrast of the children's joy in life, their laughter and involvement, and my feeling of rejection and that I was the target of evil forces seemed ridiculous. Beauty was turned on its head. Something was going on that I didn't understand. Something about ghosts.

NB Now that I am looking back on our time on the island I realise that it was the start or rather the trigger of what is commonly known as a mental or nervous breakdown. I had suppressed my fear from the nearly fatal rupture from my mother. It was on the island that I realised her betrayal and the injury she had done me. My vulnerability was back. The Devon sojourn, though long ago, was undoing me. The next few years I doubled my efforts to make my children feel loved and safe, worried the while that I might do them psychological harm, and at the very worst abandon them. Ghosts, ghosts.

The breaking point came when another buried memory resurfaced. We were living in London at 56 Marlowe's Lane and were giving one of our dinner parties when we often danced and continued drinking into the small hours. I was sitting on the knee of, I forget his name, but I know he was in the diplomatic service, and he had an erection. I can still remember my feeling of horror and danger. Of course I behaved as if there were nothing untoward, but that night my legs felt strange and in the morning I couldn't walk or stand. My legs were paralysed. I showed no concern, which is one of the traits of the condition, and was smartly whisked away to hospital as it was thought that I had polio. After tests, including a lumbar puncture, it was decided that my paralysis was hysterical and I was moved to a hospital specialising in mental disorders.

I won't go into too much detail, but I absolutely refused to have shock treatment, and after a week of medication and talking to a psychiatrist I slowly was able to walk again. I played a lovely game of croquet with a dishy young doctor on the day I left. I was a little wobbly at the start, but my balance was restored the more I got involved. So that was the start of three years of therapy; of healing through remembering, understanding and facing the ghosts. Look-

ing back this breakdown was the best thing that could have happened to me. At my ripe old age of sixty-nine I realise how necessary and valuable our shit times are; it is through experiencing and living them we grow. Plants grow better when manure is dug into their soil. I discovered that it was in writing poetry that I found expression and clarity. Luckily my analyst Erik was a great lover of poetry. I subjected him to a lot of it!

After my analysis my attitude to sex changed. I no longer was afraid and disgusted.

Chapter Eleven
My Hut
Willow Cabin

Adoption

One of my clients is considering adopting as she is infertile – a state she has found difficult to come to terms with. She is concerned that she will not be a good mother as in a way she will be only acting the part. She has brought up the nature/nurture argument and wants to know how much a role genetics plays in the make up of a person's character.

Of course all this stirred up my feelings and questions about John's and my parenting and our three children. As is the custom my client knows nothing of my personal life.

So here I am in my hut pondering adoption.

I don't seem to have many negative feelings generated by the adoption experience although at the time I felt it unjust that I couldn't conceive.

I remember that for a while I thought of myself as a pariah. Not for long though.

When the children were about five or six years old we told them their adoption stories and all the little that we knew about their birth parents and the reasons that they could not keep them and why we wanted to have them. Since then they have always been open about being adopted, in fact sounding a little pleased with their lot!

They, Timmy, Richard and Caroline, are now in their late thirties, married with children of their own. And seemingly with no ill effects. I think having the three of them was beneficial as they had a lot in common and felt quite 'normal', not different. I realise that I never looked at the possible psychological harm that could have been done – in fact it didn't enter my head. I thought the great gift of being given three babies positive, challenging and a great joy. Tiring though!

But now, partly because of my client and my aroused curiosity, I have been reading a lot on the subject. I decided I would ask Richard if we could have a talk about adoption and was surprised he was glad to do so. I wondered why we had seldom talked about it. Had we made it a taboo subject? Was it really hardly relevant? Or of little consequence?

I recorded our talk, and have not edited it. I typed it out and have it with me.

I am S., and Richard is R.

S. Funny that we have hardly ever talked about adoption.

R. Not with you or Dad, but Caroline and I have quite often. Particularly about whether to meet our real mothers.

S. Which you haven't. Do you remember I did tell you I wouldn't mind if you wanted to. By the way I know it is just a word, but it upset me a little when you used the word real just now. I think of myself as your real mother.

R. Just semantics, Mum. But unlike Caroline and me Timmy did meet his mother. Only once. Actually they decided that was enough. He was pleased to have done it. He also met his half brothers, and said they looked a lot like him, although they had a different father. She had not stayed with Timmy's.

S. I didn't know. (*pause*)

R. He didn't tell you, as although you said you wouldn't mind he thought you would. He felt he was being disloyal.

S. Oh! (*pause*) Are you in any way sad that although we said you were our chosen baby, it could also be said that you were your birth mother's unchosen one?

R. Not really because you explained how impossible it was to be a single parent nearly forty years ago. I do know that I would never abandon Anne (*his wife*) or my kids. It seems a dangerous thing to do. We three were lucky to survive it.

S. Survive it? What's the it?

R. It, it – not sure but it seems a risky thing to do – to take someone away, permanently, and place them with complete strangers.

S. We were very carefully selected. The adoption society was meticulous.

R. Must say it worked out right for us; you and Dad have been – here you are Mum – real parents. (*we laugh*)

S. Do you feel disadvantaged being adopted?

R. I would have preferred to be with my real mother and father if only their situation had been different – sorry, there I go again! I find birth mother, biological mother too technical – clinical. You know there's something truly life-giving in that our children are a result of our love making; that they spent, I think I've got it right, forty weeks in Anne's womb, and that she fed them. Mum, I hope this isn't upsetting you?

S. Yes, a little. No, not really. I am all right. Of course you feel like that. Slight sadness though. In a way I was adopted, being a ward of court, but neither of my guardians became my parents. I did feel abandoned, angry and frightened. But then I was about seven years old, not a tiny baby. I think I was an imposition. You three were quite the opposite – really wanted. (*R. gives me a hug I feel quite emotional*) The so called experts say the post natal separation from a biological mother is an extreme trauma that stays in the child's subconscious – indeed throughout life and if not recognised and addressed the delayed grief can lead to acting out – aggressive behaviour, substance abuse. Also adoptees will always protect themselves from loss and separation.

R. That's balls, Mum. Most people find separation and loss difficult. I think a lot of you being a psychotherapist, but not of these theories.

S. They're not mine.

R. It sounds like the shrinks are drumming up business, a new category of fuck ups! Not worrying and just getting on with us being a family seemed to keep us sorted out.

S. They –

R. – the great analytical they –

S. – also say that adoptees may have trouble with their identity. Do you? Do you have a good idea of who you are?

R. Think so. Most people spend a lifetime trying to find out. Am I like my father, uncle, aunt? Am I this that or the other? Somehow we adopted ones can start from scratch, and just become as we go along. Authentic.

S. That's what I think too. For you it is easier to evolve genuinely, and no need to spend a lot of life discarding inherited traits that are not true you.

R. We may be a family that adoption worked well for.

S. There are quite a few that don't.

R. I think the schools we went to helped.

S. Good old Froebel. They certainly foster individuality.

R. Loving parenting is what works regardless. Parents who choose good schools. And the violin for me, rugger for Timmy, dance and swimming for Caroline.

S. We're sounding smug. We've certainly had our wobbles. Me particularly.

R. I am curious about genetics. I am going to do some studying. Interesting subject. (*pause*) I am who I am.

S. Me too – am who I am.

R. I would like to know that my first mother is OK. She was, from what you told me, greatly caring, loving, in that she wanted to give me a stable and better life than she could provide. She was young, a teenager. It must have been hard giving me away.

S. Very hard. I was so touched by the baby clothes she knitted for you. (*pause*) Interesting isn't it that few fathers are searched for. It's nearly always the mother. You'll see when you're into genes that the father plays a fifty per cent part. Come to think of it it's not so surprising – the mother is the prime carer for the first few years.

R. You told me my father was at uni. Third year, studying architecture. I like knowing that.

S. I am so glad we're having this talk. You know Rich, sometimes my profession pisses me off; often creating problems – not clever at all. (*pause*) I never even managed to come to terms with the Oedipus complex. Adoption is being made into a complex; Adoption complex. Oh, dear. (*pause*) I loved the play Oedipus Rex. Saw it with your father in Greece and in Greek. Couldn't understand a word. (*pause*) Shall we stop now? (*we did*)

I am glad to have written about a positive outcome to adoption. I feel good that I with my dodgy personality did no harm to my resilient children – in fact it affirms my belief that a bit of difficulty adds a spice to living, in fact enhances it. I wish some of the therapeutic profession would stop digging so deep and so obscurely – next thing will be 'in the womb therapy'. Why not? Why not open up a new market?

Am I becoming a bit cynical? Only about some in my

profession – and come to think of it about the pharmaceutical industry, and health and safety, and vitamin supplements, and… and… the list could become pretty long, so I'll stop.

I should not have put that word only.

I prefer to think of myself as a realist, not a cynical person.

I do love Richard.

Chapter Twelve
My Roof
The Sky

Throughout my life I have spent as much time as I could close to nature. I am putting this chapter here because the children were so often with John and me on our ventures and have inherited from us our love, fascination, awe and worship (that's a bit over the top, but true in my case) of the natural world.

As a child in Devon it was the sea that intrigued me; how welcoming it could be swimming out round the rock in the bay, how it could turn dangerous, thrilling, as Gill and I would have to stand back so the high and curving wave could not grab us.

I loved the rock pools, the little scuttling crabs, the sea-weedy smell and popping the bladder wrack. I was glad to have made close friends with the three fisherman who worked from that bay. They were called Stadden, Jake and Big Ben. They had a little hut where they kept all their fishing gear and a stove with the always bubbling kettle. The tea they offered us was very dark, and we sweetened it with saccharine, because sugar was rationed. We pre-tended to like it, but didn't. It was a friendly thing for them to do. They made us feel welcome.

They often took us out fishing, mostly for mackerel. We each had a line and one part of me dreaded the tug that told me a fish was hooked. I didn't want to kill but I wanted to be one of the lads and it was exciting. Just look at the fish I have just caught! The radiant silver, the blue sort of green, the intricate design of the scales entranced me – and watching the brilliance fade as my fish died made me feel a sadness, a sort of weighty sadness that I hadn't experienced before.

We sometimes got a dogfish; it seemed very large, ugly and a miserable colour; it thrashed around the bottom of the boat taking a long time to die. Gill and I lifted our legs out of the way, and put them on the side of the boat. It was horrid to see it suffer and it felt as if it was angry with us and would like to strike us. Sometimes one of the men would pick it up by the tail and whack its head, and it would be stilled. I didn't think humans ate dogfish but I believe they were made into cat food. Cat eats dog!

We also picked up the lobster pots and lifted the lobsters out and put them in the buckets we had with us. They needed to be kept alive for they were sold that way. A cook would plunge them into boiling water so that it was known that they were fresh. Gill and I had heard that the lobster screams when put in the boiling water, but Stadden who was the lobster cooking specialist (they sold quite a lot of them already cooked) informed us that the scream was the steam escaping from the shell. We were not convinced. They, in their blue black shells, fascinated me, miniature sea monsters with primeval movement and great pincer claws.

When the weather was stormy or the sea too rough we would help make the lobster pots. Big Ben was in charge. They used switches of willow, reed or bamboo. It was hard bending the wood, and weaving it into the right shape. Even if the willow was green it really was too hard for us to handle – so when I say we helped, we mostly brought

71

them mugs of tea – and us admiring their basket making craft really chuffed them.

In bed at night with my window wide open I could hear the ocean murmur and it comforted me and dispelled my loneliness.

John liked to sail and for a while we had a forty-two foot ketch. We would spend much of the Spring and Summer school holidays sailing, mostly in the Mediterranean.

We became, I already was, respectful of the sea; its strength and beauty, its danger and its complete indifference to us. We were not like the dolphins who seemed befriended by it. We loved it when one of us sighted a dolphin, or perhaps a school. We would rush up on deck to enjoy the Dolphin Dance.

At night it was the sky. An unclouded night sky. Different worlds wheeling and whirling, each in its appointed place. The shooting stars were good navigators and never hit a target, anyway as far as we could see. The Milky Way, a celestial river. And the majestic full moon, growing from a silver sliver then shrinking back to it, then growing from it again with such time keeping and seeming patience. Waxing and waning.

Woods. As a family we always arranged a time and place to meet after our woodings, but to experience a wood we felt we needed to be alone. On your own to choose your way, your pauses, your listening: the rustle of leaves, the creak of a branch. Bird song.

On your own to look, to be surrounded by trees, each one a magnificent work of art. Their symmetry, their motion when moving in the wind, the colours changing throughout the year and the exquisiteness of their winter nakedness.

Gill and I shared this passion for trees and we often went on walks together and had no need to separate and be on our own because we didn't impose on each other and had no need to communicate – just experience. I had been and was still learning the trees' Latin names because I wanted to be in touch with their past, and give them prestige by naming them.

We were proud that our family crest was an oak tree (Quercus). Gill would research the trees' origins, and that is what we talked about afterwards, but never the feelings, often spiritual ones, that were evoked.

One impulse from the vernal wood
can teach you more of man,
of moral evil and of good
than all the sages can.

Wordsworth

Sometimes a great poet and even when not, like in the above piece, his ideas and beliefs resonated with mine. Pantheist, nature worshipper.

It was the same with the family. We kept off feelings and the spiritual and would discuss practical things: Timmy wanted to find the best wood for carving and for making cricket bats. Richard, always a bit of a boy scout like his father, wanted to know wood lore – he had got lost one time and it had scared him. Caroline, interested in alternative medicine, wanted to find plants or trees with medicinal qualities, but like her father and me, was happy to just be in the woods.

There was a day when I might say I wasn't totally happy. I got lost. We were in what they call a managed woodland with many varieties of tree. My interest that day was in ants and I was looking for a nest. I knew that they liked to be in a clearing where the warmth of the sun could reach them. I also knew that they needed aphid bearing trees close to them so that they had a good supply of honeydew. Ants interested me a lot because our family motto was Ite ad Fornicam – Go to the Ant (from *Proverbs*); the sentence continues 'learn from its ways and be wise'. I liked to think it meant Go Fornicate. I was engrossed, moving from one clearing after another. I didn't look at my watch until I at last found what I was looking for. A sort of dome shaped pile of twigs and leaves with little trails to the trees nearby. Eureka, until I saw the time.

It was almost an hour after I was meant to meet the family. And where was I? Lost.

I said I wasn't totally happy that day as I didn't want the children and John worried about me, but in truth I had a feeling of elation and revelation. It was great that the wood had won, it was great that the ant nest was out of the reach of prying humans, it was great that I was alone with the ants. I was happy! I decided to stay put and concentrate on the movement of ants and see what turned up. And what did turn up was Scatty, our lovely scatterbrained dog. She guided me back to our meeting place and when we got there her tail wagged so widely and strongly I thought she might lose her balance.

What a day! I was told I was a bad example – this was especially from Caroline, so I promised to do better. The heroine of the day was Scatty and she knew it.

I had liked being lost, which surprised me; perhaps it was because being found is reassuring and proof of some-thing – maybe love.

I wondered whether ants had a system so they always knew their whereabouts, perhaps carrying a map in their heads. I needed to 'learn from their ways and be wise'. Something I'd like to add here – all worker ants are female. Ha!

I have never yet been in a forest, but hope to one day.

The countryside. Although I have lived my whole life in London we spent most of our holidays (apart from sailing) in the country. We stayed on farms, the children often camping. I loved the patchwork of fields, the scent of the wheat, the cider smell of fallen apples, the delicacy of those apple trees in Spring, generously dressed in pink and white. All those wild flowers that I had known since childhood and could name. Plantains to play soldiers – the winner being the one who knocked their opponent's head off first. Does someone like butter? Put the butter-cup under their chin and see if there is a yellow reflection. Does he love me? love me not? Picking the petals off a daisy, the last petal representing the truth. Sometimes we spoke it in French, as the game Effeuiller la Marguerite originated in France. Il m'aime? Pas du tout. We all cheated, I think, and manoeuvred the picking to get the reply we wanted.

Blackberrying and making jam. Blackberry and apple crumble. Collecting the eggs laid by those shiny chestnut coloured Rhode Island Reds, and from the ducks. Why are the females so dowdy? Why the males so colourful ? Why is it the opposite in us humans?

Drinking warm milk from those gentle Jersey cows, luxuriating in their cream (very good with apple crumble) and sometimes eating homemade cheese which John and I learnt to make. How well these animals provided for us.

There was one farm dog named Patsy who was a local champion in the sheepdog trials. Impressed with Patsy we had one of her puppies, which got us walking in Richmond Park – but we never got her to do more than come when we called her (not always) and sort of momentarily sit when we said sit. We named her Scatty. We didn't have the patient ways of nature and those who work with it, so we rushed the training. She must have been muddled having five masters and so felt justified to do whatsoever she liked!

Gardens. In Marlowe's Lane we had quite a large one for London. We started from scratch, rather John did. I had ideas and drew the design, which wasn't adhered to. The garden improvised itself, the major part of it being a lawn. There was a magnificent Mulberry tree whose berries stained our clothes – permanently, nothing could get out those dark red marks – and one smaller tree in which was perched a tree house made by the children. No adults permitted. A great place to smoke your first cigarette.

I enjoyed choosing the shrubs and perennials, weeded and watered, but did none of the heavy work.

We did visit some National Trust gardens hoping to be inspired. I recall Sissinghurst Castle partly because its owner, Vita Sackville-West, was a poet (a not very good one, on the fringe of the Bloomsbury Group). She had created the gardens with her historian husband, Harold Nicholson. A poet and a historian – a little like us. It had, as far as I can remember, seven different gardens each with a theme. There was the white garden, the herb garden, the rose garden, the cottage garden. Cultivated gardens, some of them informal, but so human-made that I felt I was not in nature, but nature had been used as if it were from a palette of paint making a picture. Give me a wilderness any time!

As a reaction to these beautifully kept and conceived gardens I decided to let ours run wild, which it enjoyed doing. We did cut the grass, trimmed plants back if they got out of control and watered them when need be. It was a beautiful garden. We should have entered it for the Chelsea Flower Show, under a new category, Wilderness Gardens.

Richmond Park. We spent a lot of time there. It is a

wonderful place to be. It is large and varied. There is the Henry VIII mound, which is thought to be a barrow from the Bronze Age, from which to survey St Paul's cathedral – with the help of quite a powerful telescope. There are coppices and woodland, ancient parkland trees some reaching back to the time when Charles the First hunted there. There is wetland, bogs, bracken, and grassland. Enclosed inside the park is the Isabella Plantation. We would go there in late Spring to breathe in the exotic perfume of azaleas and feast our eyes on their colours and those of the rhododendrons.

There was space in the park for long walks, special spots for picnicking, fields for football, ponds for floating boats and feeding the overfed ducks.

This reads like a publicity blurb. Richmond Park is quite a park! An example of how humans can nurture nature.

I can't believe it, I forgot to mention the deer, and I forgot to mention the birds, over fifty different varieties.

I have a feeling of kinship with nature. I feel worshipful. One long silent WOW.

NB Writing down these different encounters with nature, and admitting that I felt a sense of worship, tells to me that I might have been equating nature with God.

you are progressing

A WOW, even a silent one, I now realise is a sure sign that something spiritual is going on. Since the deaths of Gill and Samuel I haven't been to the park, or, come to think of it, to the Henley woods, or out to the countryside. I cut myself off from something

me

as their deaths cut themselves off from me.

incorporate them

I think my grieving is abating.
    Here is a poem I wrote for children, dedicated to Stadden, Jake and Big Ben. It is in gratitude to them befriending me, and teaching me quite a lesson. Just in case you wondered why they hadn't been called up, Stadden and Big Ben were too old and Jake suffered from epilepsy; we never saw him have a fit. As fishing was considered essential in providing us all with food, they were excused enlistment anyway.

When I was eight
The fisherman said
'You swim well now
So you can take
The small boat out
For I can tell
You won't fall in
I've trained you well

'Pull equally hard on you left oar and right
And above all don't you ever take fright.
Keep calm and know where you are going.
Don't give up if you wobble, just keep on rowing.'

I stepped in the 'Little-Un'. It rocked high and low,
So I sat well centred and started to row.
I was fit and well taught and filled up with hope.
As my balance was good, so was the boat's.
I was the engine, and I chose the way;
Round the rock, past the buoy, and out in the bay:
Then back to the beach. Ben, Stadden and Jake

Were there with hot cocoa, advice and hands shakes.
'You're quite a lad, girl, and when you grow up…'

I am grown-up now, and try to impart
What I experienced then, the fisherman's art
Of security, even on dark choppy seas.

I need to keep practising what I preach
But they instructed me well on that red Devon beach.

I read the other day that experiments in an Irish university
have shown evidence that crustaceans feel pain. A dilemma
for me as lobster with good mayonnaise is my favourite meal.
Have tests been done to see if fishes feel pain? It cer-
tainly looks as if they do; all that thrashing about as they
slowly die. Imagine the hook in the fish's mouth and the
agony when it is yanked out, as it so often was. Imag-
ine the agony of asphyxiation caused by being out of the
water, their element.
I certainly hope there will be proof that they are imper-
vious to pain.

Chapter Thirteen
56 Marlowe's Lane

John and I and the children lived here until Caroline finished university; she studied medicine, and is now a GP. We always had help, either an au pair or someone full time. We also had a daily who was practical and motherly with the children, and a confidante to me on all things parenting. We were happy. John and I had interesting careers. I didn't start working until Caroline was two. My work was varied and part time. I brought money in by teaching theatre and voice in colleges and schools, and coaching at home. What I enjoyed the most was performing poetry (I can't find the right word. It would be awful to perform a poem). Perhaps speaking poetry is better. There were three of us, Natalie, David and me. I had met the two of them when I directed Milton's 'Comus'. I had cast Natalie as the Virgin (some virgin!) and David as Comus. This masque is not everybody's cup of tea, but we got good audiences, and not only made up of our friends! Some of the poetry is magnificent.

We did other poetry shows; I thought up the themes and we all researched the poems. The first one we did was 'People through Poetry' from Chaucer to the Beatles. We took it to colleges and schools, and to the general public – not really the general public, a specific public. It seems not many people like poetry. We had a great time and were thrilled when The British Council invited us to do a tour in France. In fact they commissioned us to do 'People Through Poetry' and an ecological programme called 'No Dodo', which we had already done at the Natural History Museum in London. So we had quite a busy time for a couple of years. Rotten pay, but a creative and blissful time. The British Council booked the tours, which were mostly in universities around and in Paris.

After that I and an actor did the same tour with 'Sex, Society and the Stage'.

He thought up the title saying sex always gets an audience. In reality there was very little sex in the six scenes we did from a selection of plays of the genre comedy of manners, perhaps a little flirtation. We started with Congreve and ended with Joe Orton.

During this time when the children were still at school I started my psychotherapy training, and worked as a child care officer as a volunteer. I was appointed a school, a comprehensive one in a disadvantaged area. They had many problems such as disruptive behaviour, unpunctuality, and truancy, and very low exam results. Quite a few of the kids were badly nourished or exhausted (often from watching television to all hours) and seemed on the edge of being ill. The staff selected the children who needed the most help and my job was to go on a home visit and hopefully get the parents or parent to co-operate with me in sorting things out. Most of the families lived in flats in large tall ugly blocks, with minimal sized concrete-plus-a-bush-or-two gardens. There was a certain smell in the stairways, sort of uncared for smell – the same description could be applied to the children I was hoping to help. I was nearly always welcomed in and offered a cup of tea. For the most part the mothers I visited were single, or with an often absent father. They were poor, practically uneducated, sometimes illiterate, not working and living off benefits. Many of them had three or four children and it was all too much for them to cope with. They felt overwhelmed and had very low self-esteem. They just did not have the energy or knowhow to help themselves or their children. Each one of them said they wanted the best for the children but were stuck, and didn't know what to do. The parent of a truant was usually unaware that school was being missed, and anyway what could she do about it. (I am sure she was thinking what the hell had school done for her.) Especially difficult were the boys; some of them were hanging out with one of the local gangs, maybe already into drugs, and could be intimidating.

To get a good relationship with the parent or parents was my main concern, and in most cases I succeeded. I think I came across as non judgemental, caring for her (as I said, it was usually the mother) as well as the children. But what was to be done?

There was no quick fix, so the head teacher, Mrs Barry, and I worked out a strategy.

We would enrol and train volunteers to take on a few families and help them.

Here is a list of what we could do if needed or felt of benefit.

- Arrange for someone to accompany the child to school, and possibly home after school giving an opportunity to talk about homework and even help with it.
- Have regular meetings, off the school premises, in which to show an interest in their aspirations and their education.

- Arrange out of school activities, whether sport, music, pottery, you name it.
- Visit the mother, with luck alongside the father, at least once a term and show an interest in all members of the family.
- If there were medical, psychological or addiction problems get them attended to.
- In addition to Parent Evenings the school would invite parents to a friendly and entertaining happening once a term. Films were the most popular.

I and Tony an actor friend formed a theatre group, and we put on a review. There were over twenty kids in it, and they wrote a lot of the material. This show, called 'Higgledy – Piggledy', was one of the happenings we invited the parents to. The school had a large community hall with a stage and some lighting; we rented in a couple of spot lights. I well remember a couple of real tearaway boys being in charge of the lights, spots and all; they were highly efficient and artistic, and they loved it.

It was a success, enthusiastic singing (Tony played the piano) and satire. It was a little vulgar at times, but often funny and moving. My favourite scene was when the boys did a ballet wearing tutus – it was hilarious. In addition to the actors we had wardrobe, make-up, scene painting and stage hands. It was a real group endeavour.

This was a time when my social conscience got awoken. I was deeply shocked at the inequality I witnessed. It made me count my blessings and encouraged me to qualify as soon as possible in psychotherapy. The psychological problems these troubled kids and parents had could only be helped slightly by us volunteers – better than nothing though.

They needed counselling at the very least. And the schools needed to brighten up.

NB I nearly didn't look back on this time as I thought my life was run of the mill, but by writing about some of it I realise how valuable much of it was.

I learnt how to communicate with kids from all walks of life; there were my three and their privileged and cultured friends, and the deprived school children from the tower blocks, disadvantaged, insecure and ill educated. Mrs Barry, the head teacher, was admirable in trying to elevate the educational standard and in introducing pastoral care and extra curriculum subjects. She had no financial resources to pay for these services and had to count on volunteers.

After all these years I hope these initiatives are still carrying on because they helped a lot. From what I gather state education is still pretty dire. The school was shabby and needed more than a coat of paint. The playground was a concrete disgrace. Not a touch of colour or nature anywhere. Not even a tree. Uninspiring, a depressing environment. Who would want to be there? Why bother? They haven't bothered. Most depressing. I was pleased to get to know some of the children and to meet their parents, and to work with Mrs Barry, but knew that we were whistling in the wind. Too many hurdles: not enough money, too large classes, lack of discipline, lack of fun, sport, good food, and unfortunately a paucity of good teachers. I had imagined the literature shows and the reviews were indulgencies. Sort of icing on the education cake. I am now aware of how important the creative arts are. How much better you learn if you are enjoying yourself, at the same time as being introduced to well expressed ideas from feelers and thinkers.

Particularly valuable when a feeler and thinker happens to be you!

Chapter Fourteen
56 Marlowe's Lane

We, my husband John and I, moved into this Edwardian very large house because we wanted to have at least three children. It was a horrible time for me, as I couldn't get pregnant. I had all the tests and there was nothing wrong at all except I produced some type of acid that killed off the sperms so that they never reached an ovary. I found myself unable to go to our friends' children's christenings or parties, I just burst into tears. The state I was in didn't help our pleasure in love making, not that I liked the whole thing much anyway, it was too intrusive – I had to douche with something to counteract the acid, and directly after coitus, as the gynaecologist clinically called it, lie with my legs up in the air to improve the angle of my vagina, but to no avail and not very erotic!

After about two difficult years, we decided to adopt and things immediately changed for the better. There were many babies for adoption at this time. Contraception was not 100% reliable, condoms for the men, which they were unhappy with as they were not easy to apply (and more than often didn't) and cut down on sensitivity and sensation. For women the choice was between a diaphragm 'insert it each night just like cleaning your teeth and use a generous amount of the spermicidal jelly'. What a foreplay! When I was not wanting to become pregnant I used this method and hated to imagine the murderous poison working inside me. Or they could be fitted with a coil; not for me as I saw the coil like a venomous snake poised to strike. However, all this was behind us – trying not to and trying to have a baby.

We went to an agency and they came and saw our home, and interviewed us many times. We were told we could have up to three babies spread out over the next few years. They said they would do their best to match our colouring, physiques and backgrounds. London was awash with babies.

One day the telephone rang and it was the agency. 'We have a beautiful three weeks old baby boy, and he will be here tomorrow afternoon at two o'clock. Could you bring a carry cot to take him home with you.' I had never had a headache but I got one. I was thrilled but apprehensive, hoping that I could be a wonderful mother to him, and that he would be happy to be our son. It was an unbelievably poignant moment when I first saw him. Something warm and vibrant passed between us. I lifted him from his carrycot and held him close.

He smelt and felt so good.

'you arrived round and strong
with large clear eyes'

We were told that his father was a student and a good sportsman, and his mother training to become a teacher. We discussed practical things like how many ounces of milk he should take and how often, including one feed in the small hours. O dear!

' you drank and eat heartily'

The adoption would become legal after six months, giving his birth parents time in case they should change their minds and want him back. Timothy, the name we gave him, and I became close. Looking into each other's eyes we could read what each of us needed. I needed affirmation that I was a good mother, so that my imagined inheritance that I was to be a bad parent might be dispelled, and he that his thirst for food, need of movement and closeness would be provided. He loved the time he spent with his father. He hardly ever cried, but seemed to have a lively sense of humour and marvellous sort of chuckle.

I could go on and on about this adopted child. It was the building of an intimate relationship, based on mutual love. I felt blessed that I had been given such a precious life to help grow, and to find out that I had the capacity to love and be loved.

Each year we adopted another baby and the experience of wonder was just the same. Each baby was uniquely beautiful but with different needs and different ways of growing. So two boys and a girl, Timmy, Richard, and Caroline. We were a family. I had a family at last.

I haven't gone into the exhaustion bit, the lack of sleep, the endless nappies, sterilising bottles, the mashing up of vegetables and fruit. By the time we adopted Caroline an efficient nappy service had come into being, and jars of pureed baby food came on the market, and so did washing machines; we bought one, which saved time and effort, although we still had to put everything through a wringer and then hang the washing out, or in the winter put it on the radiators.

I did have help in the shape of au pair girls, and a motherly daily, Mrs Scott, who was practical and loving. We were all very lucky and our big house seemed filled to its happy brim.

My writing and teaching went on the back burner, but
I did write this poem about Timothy when he was about
six years old and had just made his clay model.

You arrived round and strong
with large clear eyes
pushing for independence from the start
You drank and eat heartily
dared danger in trees and on roofs
risked speed on your tricycle
and never lost your head
your movement free and beautiful

One day you moulded out of clay
a perfect child-Christ
astride a dinosaur
He rode there balanced calm
His head mounted on a pin
so that it moved full circle
to observe the world
This prehistoric beast's four hoofs
plonked squarely on the ground

There you sat aloof and safe
I prayed that nothing would ever topple you
or take away
the certainty that you had that day

So, three children legally ours with only our surname,
Benson, to be lumbered with. I thought they were freer
than birth children. No admonishments – 'you must have
got that from Granny' 'Just like your Uncle, you'd better
be careful' 'Not surprising when you think of what hap-

pened to…' 'You inherited that!' They were especial and created themselves; authors, not copies.

I'm happy to think that they may have picked up a few good traits from John and me; like us they enjoyed talking, and seemed to have liberal thoughts, curiosity and a great interest in learning. And our bad traits?

That was the nurture bit, and the nature bit I really didn't think about. I did not believe the make-up of their characters had much to do with inheritance or genetics – not that we knew all that much about their biological parents. Each child in my opinion had its own autonomous nature. I felt that not only because of them, but because I and my sister had not become drunks or addicts in any sort of way and our parents were an alcoholic genetic whammy!

I will leave us there, Timmy is six and a half, Richard five, and Caroline is nearly four. I love them dearly.

NB I realise that the three children were just as much part of me, related to me, as had they been conceived in my womb. I now know, or think I know, that all of us are more than related, we are in some way one. I have an expansive feeling. My family is getting amazingly large!

you are waking up

I feel that I am slowly moving out of my torpor. I think I would like to write a book, a play or poems about waking up. I think I would like to do so, but

but me no buts

as I often say to my clients it is a good sign when you say you are going to do something, not would like to, nor, I am thinking of doing so and so.

practise what you preach

I have decided to take my own advice. So here goes.

Extract from 'Waking Up'

Observe minutely the bee
breaking the silence
between
five petalled suns
that shine for one day only
Register the sounds
from buzz to scraping bark
echoed in cracked voices of old men
All creation is from one pot
sounds colours smells and bodies
the lot.

I am going to get writing again.

attagirl

I feel encouraged.

Our three children are parents themselves now. I would like to talk to them about inheritance and what they think about it. There are seven grandchildren, none of them adopted. I haven't included them in this autobiography because there are enough stories to fill another book! Of course they played and play a great part in John and my lives. I sounded strident and opinionated about the subject of adoption in the piece you've just read. Now that I have had analysis and am a psychotherapist my thinking about it and many other things has changed. I do think, but am not totally convinced that one's nature has something to do with genetics, with inherited traits. I do just wonder if I was sterile because I didn't want to repeat or be a mother like mine, and that is why I produced that killer acid. That would prove at a deep level that already I credited inheritance. So this for me is another don't-know-for-sure area – there are more and more of those as I get older, and hopefully wiser. Not to know is freeing and brings along a feeling of faith and energy. It is exhilarating not being shackled by tenets and convictions.

When Timmy was about sixteen he said he didn't understand how his mother could have abandoned him. He was pretty angry. I told him that much had changed since he was born. In those days you could not be an unmarried mother and live on your own; it was more than frowned upon. It was not like now when the state will help getting a flat and gives other allowances too. Society's attitude has gentled. Quite right. I understood his feeling well. I had to have help to find my hurt and anger with my mother. It took a while to acknowledge those feelings as I wanted the receiver of my love to be perfect and marvellous. She wasn't, I am not, and I love her.

I wish I had spoken earlier and more openly to Timmy about the circumstances surrounding adoption. After our talk I made a point of telling Richard and Caroline the situation unmarried mothers found themselves in when they were born, and what a loving thing it was for them to put them out for adoption. I had thought John's and my parenting and our family life would make the children feel completely integrated, settled and secure – but not so.

Chapter Fifteen
21A Lifton Road

I lived here after I had left the Royal Academy. A tiny furnished flat but it was all I could afford as I now had to make my own way. I had teaching jobs, voice and drama. These were in a private school in Guildford, an art college in Gravesend and in a cooking school in Victoria. I had a small group that came to my flat where we worked on public speaking. One guy was from a Scottish whisky family and needed to make speeches to promote his brand. We always had a wee dram at the end of the evening. It became my favourite drink, and I liked it neat.

I loved teaching and was good at it. The girls from Guildford won many prizes and certificates for verse speaking and acting, and got to enjoy storytelling, and stories of all kinds. So my work programme was full and my income just about sufficient.

I was consciously looking for a husband. I still wasn't interested in love affairs, but was trying to be less of an Ice Maiden. However, I was still determined to remain a virgin until I was married. It wasn't so rare in those days to think like me. Even at the Academy only one girl in my year slept with her boyfriend. The trouble was I was attracted to sexy men, men who had been around and were sexually practised. I hoped to find someone who loved the theatre, literature, nature, had an interesting job, who had a good income and a curiosity about life, who liked to dance, eat good food and be in love with me! I suppose I was asking a lot. So, what happens? One day I am on the underground and John gets into the same carriage as me; we are both reading *The Economist*, me because there was a review of a book that interested me (the art section is always good) and he, I noticed, an article about nuclear power. Neither of us, we were to discover later, would have even glanced at each other's choice of reading. He looked extremely patrician, already balding, his dark hair going white at the temples. He was dressed informally, with an olive green sweater over a shirt, no tie and Professor Higgins like beige corduroys. There was no affectation about him, he just was. And that's what got to me. No performance, no tricks. A real example of 'I am'.

Somehow or other we invited each other for a coffee before our upcoming meetings, mine with a play director and his with someone in the oil industry. We got off at Charing Cross. We only had twenty minutes, but that was enough for us to decide to meet that evening. We exchanged telephone numbers and he said he would be in touch after work to arrange which restaurant we'd go to. He had a lovely voice and a slight American accent, and expressive golden flecked eyes.

He didn't have most of the attributes I had hoped for in a husband; he wasn't into poetry or theatre, not much interested in psychology. His work was scientific. He was a history buff, and into world affairs. He did not dance, which was a pity, but did enjoy food and wine, and although only thirty-five was a director of an international company. He spoke French and Spanish, and his accent was because his mother was American and he had spent the war years in the States, being just too young he avoided the call-up. He was ten years older than me, and seemed content with life, and his life; he just was not complicated, not ambitious but deeply concerned about preservation and sustainability. We both were left wing.

Neither of us fell in love but we fitted, his calm sureness earthing me, and my arty and imaginative flights lifting him. He smelt right, a sure sign to me that a man is safe, so it was no problem for us to make love. I completely forgot that I was to be a virgin until married. Anyway I wasn't! The fact that he couldn't or wouldn't dance was a shame, but he loved to sail so we had a yacht and many of our holidays were in the Mediterranean. I think we visited all the islands! The tales he told us from history we all loved. There is one gruesome one that sticks in my memory – severed heads being used as cannon balls! He knew how to sail, and could navigate by the stars. At night of course! I loved him for that, particularly his intimate knowledge of the galaxy, and above all I loved him for being such a healthy natural being.

NB I have learnt so much from John: life is to be taken for what it hands out. It was no great tragedy that I couldn't conceive, let's adopt. If one of the children was making a mess of things he would try to help them sort it out, but not to flap (especially me). Things work out one way or another and we need a few messes – learning curve, don't you know. I mentioned above that whisky was my favourite drink. It still is. I have to watch it as it caused my mother's downfall.

Can alcoholism be inherited? I don't think so. I wonder how John is. I miss him.

Chapter Sixteen
Bedsitter in Kensington

I feel so grown-up, seventeen years old with my own place paid for by my father at three guineas a week. The excitement of unpacking my saucepan, steamer, frying pan, kettle and cutlery! There is only one gas burner for cooking and a small gas fire which I pay for by putting shillings in a meter I christen The Guzzler. It is a tiny room about three yards by four, right at the top of this Victorian house that has been converted into twenty bedsitting rooms by Mr Donarski, who owns and runs it. He had been in the Polish military stationed in England, and after the war he decided to settle here with his wife; life in Warsaw was untenable under the communists. I nicknamed him The Don as he was always at his desk and wore large horn rimmed glasses. I never saw him smile in the three years I lived here. I tried so hard to bring some fun and joy into his life but to no avail. Mrs Donarski never made an appearance, she seemed to be in hiding.

Back to describing my room. There is a single bed that doubles up as a sofa, a small armchair, two upright chairs, a table, a wardrobe and a wash basin in a sort of construction that conceals it when I am not using it to wash myself or the dishes.

The bathroom is downstairs and I share it with six others. There are some wall shelves on which I have my books, mostly poetry and plays, and my already well thumbed Shakespeare and *Oxford Book of English Verse*. I had to buy *An Actor Prepares* by Stanislavski as method acting is what we will be doing at the Royal Academy. I am so excited at the thought of training to be an actress and have made myself tunics – black for mime and fencing, pale blue for Greek dancing. I have ballet shoes (not blocked) and black tights and feel pleased that I have good legs – what luck! And what luck there is a lift here so that I only have to climb the last flight of stairs. I'm writing in the present to get you to feel my sense of freedom, self reliance and adventure. It is as if I am walking on air. I love my newly cut pageboy hair style and twirl around making it swing. I feel quite beautiful and sort of glowing.

I think I'll find it easier to tell you more about my student days by making four sections. London. The Royal Academy. Boyfriends. Events.

London: London was still scarred by the bombing and lacked a lick of paint. In fact it was quite shabby, but to me it was a magical city. During my first year food and clothes were still rationed as was petrol, so there were few cars; we bussed, Tubed and walked everywhere. The theatre was booming, and I spent a lot of time in The Gods (one shilling and nine pence a ticket) mostly at The King's Theatre and The Lyric, both in Hammersmith; the West End was too expensive. I saw Richard Burton as Cuthbert in 'The Boy With The Cart', which for me was the perfect mix of poetry and drama, and what a voice! That line 'I was a carpenter' at the end of the play quivered me. I shared Cuthbert's awe.

a revelatory moment poetry can awaken people extend their senses and perceptions

I felt inspired. Then and there I decided to not only be a verse speaker but a poet. In fact that very night, far into the small hours I wrote the following poem.

Tabula rasa – Ha, ha !

beyond the ha-ha lie the fields,
cattle and sheep lazily grazing,
woods and leaves alight and blazing,
fields with five-barred gates all leading
to more fields, yellow with wheat,
donkeys, thistles, four-leaf clovers,
shade and sunshine, safe lovers,
through and over stiles and hedgerows
until the world sweeps wide horizons
lifting the hills to touch the sky

I suppose I digress showing you my poems, but I really want to.

I saw 'Murder in the Cathedral' in Southwark cathedral. Eliot is a favourite of mine, he makes me think, feel and understand. I won't go into detail about all the other plays I went to as it would take up pages. I'll just list those that particularly grabbed me. 'The Entertainer'. Although I had fallen for Laurence Olivier in the film 'Henry V' he now seemed a trifle ham, but alcoholics (not Larry, well perhaps Larry, and Archie Rice) always fascinate me. 'A Streetcar named Desire'. I was both shocked and thrilled; it was raunchy and crude, but great method acting. The overt sex really offended and at the same time intrigued me; it was something new that I was only just beginning to know about – and alcoholics again. Seeing drunkenness on stage helped me to realise that my mother and father were not unique in their drinking and that it was not as frightening or rare as I had previously thought. Poor Blanche who so much wanted to stay a lady!

By the way I forgot to mention that my father died recently from cirrhosis of the liver. I didn't go to his funeral, but Gill did. I felt a bit like Cordelia, in both our cases being honest about our lack of feelings for our fathers. I couldn't care less that he was dead. Luckily my grandparents took over the cost of my training and living expenses.

'Look Back in Anger'. Kitchen sink realistic stuff about a class of people not normally portrayed on stage, and that I hadn't encountered in the elitist environment where I had found myself. There they were expressing feelings just like mine. Characters not at all Noel Coward like! I saw at least ten Shakespeare plays, my all time favourite being 'King Lear'. What poetry! 'Blow winds and crack your cheeks! Rage! Blow!' His and the storm's fury equal in force, his character psychologically spot on, or so I budding psychologist thought! Through insanity and suffering a bad king and father becomes a good man transformed through experience, acquiring wisdom and the ability to love. Watch him carrying the hanged Cordelia, his beloved daughter, in his frail arms. Maybe one day I'll get to love my dead father. Or anyone.

of all my writers shakespeare is the best at speaking me

Lear was played by John Gielgud – another actor with a beautiful expressive voice. As his friend Alec Guinness described it, 'a silver trumpet muffled in silk'.

'The Tempest' is also one of my favourites. I learnt Prospero's (played by Ralph Richardson) breaking his staff speech by heart. He forgives and is free. He doesn't need his magic or his power. He releases his enslaved helpers; Ariel his air spirit and glorious Caliban his earth spirit. What a liberation! I am far away from forgiving or loving most people in my past. Shakespeare is a shaker upper, and a mover.

he is tuned in you are too learn from us

I am influenced by his plays and poetry.

It seems that my London mainly revolves around theatre going which of course was teaching me almost as much about acting as The Academy.

The Royal Academy: imagine three whole years of doing what you love! There were twenty-five of us in each year, and the syllabus included voice, movement, mime, Greek dance, interpretation of both poetry and texts from plays, storytelling, fencing, improvisation, make-up, and of course many productions of plays. Those of us who were doing the teacher's diploma studied the history both of the theatre and of costume and we did teaching practice in schools. I went to a posh one in Harley Street. I loved teaching, and directed 'Androcles and the Lion' for their drama club. Having just written the word posh reminds me that in voice work, which we had three times a week, I was advised and helped to modify my accent. The vowels were too narrow; I sounded a bit like Princess Elizabeth! My favourite class was verse speaking. I wasn't the greatest of actresses, too uptight and too much wanting to be beautiful, but I was a very good at speaking poetry. I just loved the sounds of words. One of the best bits of advice for reading or performing poetry was the following: Feel, feel, feel, think, think, think, then pack it down.

The training in method acting was almost impossible for me; I couldn't recall emotions and reactions from my own life as I had taught myself not to remember many happenings. One afternoon we were asked to prepare ourselves to act the part of someone wanting to be reunited with a person they loved. First of all we lay down and relaxed completely as that helps to retrieve the memory better. I thought of being reunited with Mummy as a child and I started to sob uncontrollably. I immediately got up and left the room. I felt I had betrayed my mother, and anyway I couldn't bear the anguish. Better to shut down. We were asked to remember other emotional moments; any loving ones made me cry, any fearful or sexually loaded ones made me freeze; any murderous ones made me very very frightened, and I didn't want anyone to know. My only way through this was to make up the situations and memories then I could control myself – but it didn't make my acting any better. It disturbed me so much I even thought of quitting. I felt a bit of a nut case! However, I resolved it by deciding not to go on the stage but to teach, and stick to speaking poetry.

Boyfriends: I was very interested in men, but all did not go smoothly. I was immensely shy, and knew nothing about sex. In fact I had never seen a boy or a man naked. My first boyfriend was a lawyer. He had a background a little like mine – good public school, a well off family, but unlike mine his family were all alive and close to each other. His name was Chris. He had already slept with former girlfriends so was obviously puzzled by me who said I would stay a virgin until I married. We had a lovely time together, going to concerts, films and to pretty smart restaurants. Great conversations, walks in the parks, and dancing – our favourite dinner and dance place was called The Jacaranda. He used to come up to my room and we would dance, perhaps smooch would better describe it, to records on my wind up gramophone.

Eartha Kitt, Peggy Lee, Doris Day, Frank Sinatra and Bing Crosby. Often we would cuddle on my sofa, and slowly after kissing me he would caress my breast and after we had been together many weeks move his hand down between my legs and play with me there. I find that I cannot write about love making, it is too difficult. In fact the only way I could allow it in reality was to somehow detach myself from my body. I'd say 'Take Leave Sarah', to myself of course. I wouldn't let us undress as I was scared of exciting him, and I only held his hardness through his trousers. I could not, could not, could not touch his – I cannot even say the word. He was patient and sweet, but it all got too much for him, so we decided to end it. Chris was the nearest I got to loving. We were with each other for over a year.

There were quite a few others; we did things together, sometimes in a group like when we went to St Anton skiing, and to various dances, parties, and balls.

I never let anyone go further than kissing me and I heard I was nicknamed the Ice Maiden. However I was good company and looked the part. After Chris I only asked girlfriends up to my room. I wish I had married him, but it never entered our heads. Ice Maiden.

Events: I have just mentioned the balls. It was great dressing up in long frocks.

With the help of my girlfriends I made quite a few. A cheque from Aunt Elinor (she was very old now) gave me the chance to buy a bright flame coloured slinky dress from

Derry & Toms in Kensington High Street, and there was enough left over to have my hair cut by Raymond himself (drama students got cut wash and set for half price).

Mr Teasy-Weasy was his nickname, famous for dying hair bright colours, suggested he dye mine orange to match my dress. It looked spectacular and as it was The Chelsea Arts Ball we were going to, just the thing. I had my photo in *The Tatler.* Another ball I went to was at Sandhurst. It was a bit spoilt because I refused to go for a walk in the grounds, to the copse that was well known as a place for necking and canoodling. Also I went to couple of Hunt Balls, which were boring, as boring as the people were. Then there was The Highland Ball at The Dorchester; as that was with Chris I loved it. The other events were Henley, a bit posh but fun. Wimbledon, absolutely wonderful. I was awed by Drobny and Budge Patty. What a smashing game tennis is and how well they played it.

We all went to The Festival of Britain, which was meant to make us feel that as a country we had recovered from the war, or was recovering. And The Proms, a highlight each summer,

for me too music reaches me to you

up at the top of the Albert Hall – I'd go as often as I could afford it. Music, especially Mozart, lifted me somewhere, into a higher dimension.

that crazy gifted refined crude man is close to me

Thank you London for providing me with such riches. I loved my three years and I got all my diplomas. My only regret was losing Chris, we were right for each other.

NB I gave up wanting to have affairs. I had thought it the way to find out if my boyfriend and I we were meant for one another and marriage. It just was time consuming and stressful. I like the sentence I wrote about Lear, transformed through experience. I sincerely hope that is happening to me. I think I am changing, gradually!

Acting (which I started to enjoy once I had left the Academy) in which we had learnt at a deep level to become the characters we were playing was the best training for my future profession as a psychotherapist. To read about, let us say, ambition, does not get us to understand the complexities of the emotion, but becoming Lady Macbeth does. I have come a long way since those feelings of not loving or forgiving people in my past. It took a while but I can say I love my father and mother. Uncle David I have forgiven – almost, and love, not yet. I am working on it. Here is a poem which I wrote during my analysis. I certainly felt strongly, no forgiveness there.

Erik thought it quite good!

Death bed

So
once again
you've shut me up
pink skinned and plumped
fastidiously cleaned
you lie there
dying this time not drunk
no warrior you who earned his rest
but flaccid festering fucked up
it's not your fault never your fault
you're rotting inside

I smell it
as once I scented your disaffection
your sin smeared on mine and other's skin
your eyes are fish like now
that used to beg
let me in they said
and later on as now
forgive me
feebly your hand seeks mine
you are so frail I cannot say
I forgive you not
filled with your shame
I turn away

Chapter Seventeen
The Oldest Girls' Public
School in England

I can say being at this school saved my life – it sounds a bit dramatic but being there stopped me from switching off altogether. This covered the same time as I was spending most of my stress filled holidays at Pinewood, which you will read about after this.

Here I was safe and cared for. I was academically bright, although not so good at maths. The lessons got my brain ticking! I was good at sport and loved many of the other activities, my favourites being drama, musical appreciation, and art. There were only one hundred of us, aged eleven until eighteen. We were divided into Houses – I'll call them Red, White and Blue as I don't want you to be able to identify the school. On second thought I can't see why not, as I have only gratitude and praise for it. So guess away!

It was a beautiful Tudor mansion, with some new buildings – a large half with a stage, laboratories and a gym. It had housed a monastic order at some point – the carp pond was still there, with resident frogs. It had been closed by Henry VIII. At a later date a serious curse had been laid upon it concerning untimely deaths of first born sons. Awful fate befell at least three heirs, so it was ideal for a girls' school to be established there. We loved the tale and embellished it with gory stories. I wrote my first narrative poem, called *The Carruthers*, who did not heed the warning, and their son (I won't go into the glorious, corrupt, criminal details of his demise) was found O alas! disembowelled, decapitated, thrown into the carp pond with the carnivorous toads. 'Life was not merciful to Beloved Percival' was the closing line.

The grounds were huge, over one hundred and eighty acres, lovely woods and fields as well as hard tennis courts, a swimming pool (unheated and with frogs), an outside theatre space and a Dower house. Also a place called Hitler's Hall where we were to assemble if there were an invasion. It was evident that there was a war on as there was rationing of everything. It was very cold in winter for there was no coke for the boilers. We wore vests, suspender belts, thick stockings, and a garment called a spencer, why I do not know, a sort of lightweight woollen pullover underneath our shirt, then our callies (unusual name – a clue?) short for calisthenics gym slip, and a woollen cardigan, and of course our school tie with its diagonal bands of gold and green. (Have you guessed the school by now?) When it was freezing we dressed underneath our bed clothes. In the summer term we wore green and white gingham dresses with our cardigans, it never seemed that hot. And short white socks.

We each had a jam jar with our name on it: Sarah Benson. 1 oz. of butter, 2 oz. of margarine a week, which we spread on some mucklety dun coloured bread which was very tasty – there were no white or brown loaves. We had a second hand clothes and uniform shop because clothing coupons restricted what we could buy new. We bathed twice a week – water only up to the height of the side of your hand, four fingers and thumb – about four inches, otherwise we had a strip wash we called topping and tailing. We were rationed to two sweets a day after lunch, and six on Sundays before our reading siesta. We went to the local church in the morning and wore our skirts and jackets and our awful hats – the panamas were better in the summer. Each month we had a quiet hour with the headmistress and we'd discuss such things as fairness, marriage, different religions, books, and something we called moral dilemmas of which there were many! There were three different age groups, the subject matter always appropriately chosen. Here are some of the subjects we discussed: might you cheat in exams, especially if you know you could get away with it? Would you report someone who may have lied, stolen something, or cheated in exams, especially if it is a close friend? (Imagine if someone had told of my stealing those peaches, I might not have been saved from suicide. You will read about it a little further on in this chapter.) Bullying: would you tell if you were the victim, or if you knew somebody else was being bullied would you get involved to sort it out?

Christianity was the faith of the school and each morning we had assembly. Apart from school announcements there were prayers. Always some for peace and our forces in the front line, which of course included most of our fathers, and a hymn. One of us, often in anguish, played the piano – the hymn and more interestingly anything the pianist chose, from musicals to Bach. It was quite enlivening to leave the hall to 'Somewhere over the Rainbow' or if played well a Chopin mazurka or waltz. When it was my turn (I was one of the anguished) I asked a friend to join me and we chopsticked together – all the many variations that I'm sure you know. We added some extra flourishes. It went down well and even the headmistress smiled.

The school day had lessons in the morning and early afternoon with prep time included, and then two hours of sport; hockey, lacrosse or tennis in the summer. After high tea, the time was ours. Often there would be house practices: plays, dancing, or we would work on our hand-icrafts – all these for inter-house competitions. Everything was organised, but in an unobtrusive sort of way.

One brilliant piece of planning was the year after School Certificate. It was decided that there was no need to take two years to study for the Higher Certificate and so we had what was called The Year. We studied art, architecture, social history, civics, politics, economics, theatre, different religions, cooking, and we borrowed babies (I think from the village) and learnt how to bathe and care for them. We were taught to knit. (I was already quite proficient as Auntie Nen had taught my mother and me.) There was something called Dorcas, I don't remember why, and our knitting was for orphans, or for families whose fathers had been killed by the Germans or the Japanese. We learned to make clothes, and use the Singer sewing machines – we had a modern one that had a treadle so that we could use both hands to hold the garment. We were shown how to darn. We darned most of the toes and heels of our winter woollen socks. We only had a new pair when the darn became a hole.

We had ballroom dancing lessons, including jive! That got us thinking about boys, and how much more fun it would be partnering one rather than a girl. Except we knew, some of us from experience, that girls dance far better than boys. That got us talking about being with a boy, about an exciting feeling which we experienced, but couldn't define. The closest we got to it was how it felt having a 'pash' on someone, usually either a teacher or a prefect. Not that we acted upon it although we did send Valentine cards signed 'Anonymous'. However, there was The Incident, which seemed somehow linked to 'pashes'.

A prefect and a fourth former were found in bed together and were expelled. We didn't fathom out what was so bad or what they had actually done. Expulsion! We worried about what that would do to their lives in the future. The Incident. Expulsion. Shamed. They must have done something very wrong.

We had concerts at the school. Myra Hess came once. We had a Bechstein. When the London Blitz was over we went up to London to see plays – the most memorable was 'The School for Scandal' with Laurence Olivier and Vivienne Leigh. We were intrigued and excited that they were lovers in real life, whatever that meant! We worked it out that hugging and kissing like in the play were part of that sort of loving. We guessed there must be something more – but what? We were taken to exhibitions and concerts and to the film 'Henry Vth'. It was one of the first films in Technicolor, it looked great and so real. Some of us, including me, had a super-pash on Larry.

It was a wonderful year!

Only five of us stayed on for the final sixth-form year; fourteen of the class were not interested in or not up to taking Higher or university entrance.

At the end of summer term assembly for leavers the headmistress always announced the next year's head girl. This time she said she was taking a risk by appointing a bit of a maverick, but that she had confidence in her, and it was – pause, roll of drums – Sarah Benson! Wow!

I liked the sound of 'maverick', but neither I nor my friends had a clue what a maverick was, so I looked it up in the library. Unorthodox. (I had to look that up too.) Independent in thought and action. Does not go along with the group – that rang true. But the bit that affected me the most was the original meaning; stray calf or range animal separated from its mother, then branded and owned by someone else. That scared me. It sounded threatening. As I was still in the library I looked up threatening synonyms in *Roget's Thesaurus*: ominous, foreboding.

As head girl I had a beautiful panelled bedroom of my own, and enormous responsibility. So much of the well-being of the school was up to us, me and the prefects. We listened to worries, unhappinesses, sorted out bad behaviour and encouraged the faint hearted. We tried to be fair, and kind, but at the same time firm. It was an education! At the same time I was captain of lacrosse, and tennis and of Blue, my house. Also I was studying for Higher – three main subjects, History, French and English Literature, and two subsidiaries, Latin and Art. But as I loved to study, and we had such great teachers, it was pleasure and so not difficult. There was a lot to do!

To think that I might have missed out on all of that. Two years before I had stood on a ledge high up on the roof determined to jump. I had been summoned to the headmistress's study to be told that my mother had died. She had had flu but was weakened by being an alcoholic, in fact as it was put to me, she had died of drink. I hadn't seen her for years, although I had the occasional longed for letter. I could not bear the news, and that I would never see her again. It was too much. It overwhelmed me. I wanted to die, to die with her, to end it.

Then out of the blue

you can put it like that if you want

I remembered I had put two peaches I had stolen from the fruit garden in my clothes cupboard to ripen. I climbed back through the window. I found them, loved their smell and velvet softness, and cupping them in each hand pressed them to me. I sat down on my bed and ate those lovely sweet peaches, juice spilling, crying, crying. I was filled with love for Mummy. She came to be with me, and as she was with me I no longer needed to die. I don't feel I have explained this very well. She wasn't a ghost, she was just her love. I didn't understand what had happened, but it had. It felt

amor mortem vincit significant

significant.

It meant so much to me to be recognised and trusted. I was allowed to shine with no sense of showing off. Perhaps the greatest thing for me was the way my love of poetry and speaking it was encouraged. Each year there was a competition in the Friends' Meeting House in London to which a group of us always went. We won prices for the best choral speaking – psalms, T S Eliot, De La Mare, Christopher Fry, and got quite a few awards for solo verse.

B B (another clue) our drama teacher taught us well. We also took spoken poetry and drama exams, like the music ones, from grade one to grade eight, and I got the prize for the best speaker in the United Kingdom – a lovely book of theatrical historic costumes. For drama I had chosen to be Queen Anne, 'Set down, set down your honourable load' – we had to do one piece by Shakespeare.

My contemporary speech was Jennet from 'The Lady is not for Burning'.

For verse I chose a sonnet, 'It keeps eternal whisperings around desolate shores', desolate shores – desolate shores – I loved to say it. My modern poem was 'The Naming of Cats'. Ineffable effable effanineffable.

Nibble nibble edible edible – I'll use that sometime in a poem.

I decided to go to drama school not university, much to

the consternation of my grandmother but to the approval and delight of my headmistress. She made one provision, that I must take the Teacher's Diploma as well as the acting course. Some people considered that being an actress was, as a profession, decadent, a word and concept that I relished. So when asked that inevitable question, 'What do you want to be when you are grown up?' I emphasised the respectable Teacher bit. For someone of my background it was considered to be all right to become a doctor, nurse, teacher, dress designer (a bit risky) or an academic – best of all though for us girls, often pronounced gals, was to go to a Finishing School so as to be good home makers, able wives, charming hostesses – boring, boring! In these institutes they even taught the young ladies how to manage the staff, the laundry, Nanny and the children and, so very importantly, how to play bridge. My sister went to one in Switzerland where she did learn to skate, fold a table napkin (never serviette, Sarah, that's common) and make a very good cake. No shortage of butter or eggs there!

During my last term Janet, who was in our tennis team, and I played in a Junior Tournament at Queens; we represented the school but only got to the semi-finals. We had new tennis whites, pleated shortish skirts (just to the knees) and aertex shirts. We looked pretty smart! Then came a moment of glory. In the holidays we played in a County Tournament and we reached the Finals. We won and therefore qualified for Junior Wimbledon. As we had left school our headmistress who would have backed us had no more influence. My guardians (did they own this maverick?) forbade me from entering saying it was unladylike to be so competitive. I would have still been just seventeen the following year.

How ridiculous, I was not interested in being a lady. Janet's parents were all for it, but to no avail. My grandmother said they were from a different social class to us, so it was all right for Janet. Didn't I remember that I was to be presented at court? It had slipped my mind. I refused point blank. I didn't want to waste my time going to all those dances, charity balls, with chinless young men who hunted and fished. Both sports, imagine killing being a sport, I strongly disapproved. How I wished I had been eighteen, freed from guardianship – but then we had to be under eighteen to qualify for Junior Wimbledon.

I noticed I was mavericking a lot at school, even early on before I knew I was one. When the General Election chose Atlee over Churchill there was General Consternation (we thought that pretty witty) amongst most of us. Not me! Welfare State, National Health, Nationalisation, Public Education, Fair Society, Equal Opportunity. I liked the sound of it. I loved the sound of it!

In the dorm one night the conversation went like this – No more Public Schools? Nationalise this and that, including us. Reform our school! And someone said 'Gosh, that means I might have a grocer's daughter in the bed next to me – in this very dorm!' The other eight girls shared her dismay. Conservatives, snobs, each one of them! I was pleased I wanted to be with other sorts of girls; this lot, though nice, were like replicas of one other. I thought it fair that everyone should have an equal chance. What gave us the right through luck and money to hog it all. If there had been a soap box in the dorm I'd have stood on it and given an impassioned speech. But there wasn't and I didn't. For once I managed to keep my mouth shut. We were none of us sure of the facts. If they knew my thoughts I think they might have put me in 'quarantine' or 'Coventry' – a horrible isolating punishment we inflicted on each other. Nice gals not so nice!

This was the moment when I decided that I would vote

Labour when I was the right age. All the Benson family were royal blue Conservative. Maverick!

I seemed to get my ideas from somewhere inside me.

i answer to that somewhere

I did pray, mostly when walking by myself in the fields or the woods, and I'd ask the way to go, to be. I talked to the God our Christian teaching was on about,

that s me too

not to Jesus as I didn't believe he was the only son of God

you re right not the only one

or all that virgin birth fantasy stuff. I did go for his left-wing teaching, his sense of inclusion – children, outsiders, prostitutes, the villains crucified with him, even his murderers, all colours, all classes – he loved and cared for them equally.

I would never say the creed. I mouthed gobbledygook so as to look as if I were participating. If asked about religion by someone I could trust, like the headmistress, I would have said there is something outside me, inside me, I couldn't name. I was studying Wordsworth for Higher and like him might have been called a Pantheist. 'Trailing clouds of Glory' Enlightening light, enlightening poetry. I kept these thoughts to myself. I felt precocious. A little out of kilter. It would be safer to conform. Another -tic to be added to my nicknames. Heretic!

I've written down memories as they popped into my mind, not in chronological order – I hope that hasn't been confusing.

My six years at this boarding school gave me the happiest days of my seventeen year life. Wonderful schooling. Wonderful school.

Though a little sad, a little apprehensive, at the end of my year as head girl I was ready to leave and move on.

N.B. Have you have guessed the name of the school? It is still in existence. I wonder if it is so good? I'll give you another clue – the school motto which I do not like. Fortis Qui Se Vincit. I don't, and didn't then, believe we have to conquer (sounds like fighting a war) anything in ourselves. I felt that all our feelings are necessary; just that they can go any which way; we need to understand what's going on and regulate them. It seems I was already interested in psychology! Maybe I'll get in touch with the school and suggest a change in the motto – Fortis Qui Se Amat.

Being there gave me the chance to un-stereotype myself, and learn and learn. I never felt special when I did well – no great fuss was made. I was just like I was, good at many things, and it was luck.

I never included 'nibble, nibble, edible, edible' in a poem. Maybe someday.

Seeing that question what did I want to be when I grow up I remember that about twenty years ago I wrote this poem to go in an anthology for children.

1) What
she asked me
do you want to be
when you are grown up?

2) I haven't enough fingers
even including my toes
to count

the amount
of endless times
that question has been posed

3) I've thought about it deeply
and how I might reply
but one thought leads on to another
like horizons melt into the sky

4) When I am a grown-up
if that time ever comes
let me see
I'll be taller and older
a woman
and if I can make it me

Chapter Eighteen
Pinewood Lodge

Granny, my Father's mother, was one of our two official guardians, and Aunt Elinor on my mother's side the other – but she was not married and was still a practising surgeon and had no time for us, so after living in Devon Gill and I were divided up, separated; she with Aunt Lily (Granddad's sister, a rich maiden aunt who really wanted her). They lived mainly in her large house near Sunningdale golf links, and sometimes in Monk's Wall in Devon. I was to live in Pinewood Lodge, because where else? Gill and I really missed each other – we were even put in different boarding schools, she in Ascot, and me at a school in Hertfordshire. I was meant to feel proud to go there as I was the thirteenth member of the family to do so – what family? Granny and Granddad's sisters had all been there, and then their children when it had been in Ealing.

Pinewood Lodge was very big; eight bedrooms and two dressing rooms, and downstairs in the servants' quarters another three bedrooms and a sitting room. There was a large kitchen with an Aga, and larders, a scullery and a butler's pantry. Looking over the garden there was the dining room that could seat fourteen, with a conservatory leading from it, then the lovely drawing room with a music room adjoining it. Then the hall that had

117

my Grandmother's desk in the corner, and a smaller hall where the front door was, and a cloakroom that scared me with its guns, man smell, wellington boots and rain coats. There was a derelict cottage in the grounds, and a triple garage with a sitting room for the gardeners and Sidney, the chauffeur.

The grounds comprised eighteen acres and had a fenced off reserve with exotic ducks and geese and five ponds. There was Granddad's azalea and rhododendron garden, and hidden away up in the woods a heath garden.

Before the war there was a head gardener, four under gardeners and a chauffeur. Back in the house were Cook, a butler (they were husband and wife) a housemaid who lived in, and the scullery maid who came from the village. But times had changed with the war. Father Dance, (although he never did) the head gardener, and Sidney the chauffeur remained, for they were too old to enlist, and Doris came daily to clean.

As the Rolls was laid up because of the lack of petrol Sidney helped as odd job man and gardener – he was in charge of the chickens, rabbits, and pig that we kept to help out with the food rationing. He was my best friend as I loved to help him with the animals and I could talk to him.

The others in the house were my Aunt Agnes and her daughter Rosemary and quite often her son who was at Sandhurst, which was not far away, and from time to time her husband, Uncle David, would come home on leave. We also had four evacuees, but only for a short while – I think that once the doodle bugs started to come over and then the V2s it was thought better for them to move further away from London. I loved it when they were here – we had a lot of fun and I had a great time learning new words and phrases – 'Don't talk cobblers' 'Let's have a butchers'

'Sal, use your crust'. We made each other laugh, me trying to speak Cockney, and they speaking ever-so-posh. 'Dah-ling, doooo hold your knife prop-er-ly'. I thought a lot of them – because of the Blitz here they were, away from home and their mothers, but always cheerful and friendly. Rosemary didn't join in, I think she felt superior.

Pinewood was a beautiful house, with beautiful furni-ture, set in beautiful grounds. I hated it. I was frightened and alone. What sticks in my memory is not the lovely things like playing croquet on the front lawn, squash in our squash court (but not when our furniture was in store there), games of tennis on our hard court. What sticks in my memory is the happenings. And no-one to turn to.

Parallel to all this, thank heaven, was the school I went to. The thirteenth family member! Unlike most of my friends I longed for the start of term, but this chapter is about the holidays I spent at Pinewood.

So, here I am twelve years old. My hair is blonde and I brush it thirty strokes each evening before going to bed. It is lovely, silky, shiny. I put it into two plaits during the day fastening them with elastic bands, and then ribbons. I am slight, and shy about my growing bust – I now have my first bust bodice. I am a bit of a tom-boy, so am happiest when it is warm enough to wear shorts, a shirt and sandals, but most of the time it is suspender belt and stockings, a vest, pullover and skirt. As there are clothing coupons we, Rosemary and I, have few clothes.

Auntie Agnes and Granny knit us a jumper or two but mostly they make balaclavas and socks for the Forces.

My bedroom is even smaller than the dressing rooms and looks out on a brick wall – it has a small window, and is dark. Rosemary has a large room, all furnished in pink, with one of those kidney shaped dressing tables, a book shelf, a comfy chair, a long mirror, and a large window looking out over the front drive, flower beds and the start of the wood. Every evening we have our supper there – milk, an apple, and Marmite sandwiches. Then back to my room. Why was I given this pokey little room when there were so many bigger ones with lovely views? In spite of everything and what I am going to tell you, I love my room – I have my teddy bear from when I was tiny, and photos of Mummy, Gill, and Daddy, and books on my chest of drawers – mostly poetry. Also *Lamb's Tales from Shakespeare*, an Oxford dictionary, and a Latin dictionary. And my diary. It has a lock on it as it is very private and I keep the key on a ribbon around my neck.

There is a long corridor that connects the two wings of the house and my room is there. One wing is where Grand-dad and Uncle David have their bedrooms, and a spare room for visiting people like Rosemary's brother. Rosemary's room is in that wing but a little separated from the men, as are two lovely spare rooms for guests. In the other wing beyond my room is Auntie Agnes' double room with dressing room, and Granny's even bigger room and bathroom, and then beyond that Granddad's dressing room.

The point of telling you this is that the husbands slept separately from their wives and in order to visit them had to pass my door.

One evening after I am asleep my door opens and Uncle David comes in. He is very friendly and sits on my bed. He asks me about my day and strokes my hair. I do not like it, and I do not like his smell. After a short while he leavesme, and says his visits are just a secret between us. These visits happen whenever he is home on leave.

I become so nervous that I have what are called bilious attacks at least once a month. I know they are coming as I have my Big Bad Wolf nightmare. I dream that danger is coming and I have to stop it by going through a ritual

– certain words, certain gestures. I can hear the beast getting closer and closer, hear the music of 'Who's afraid of the Big Bad Wolf' getting louder and louder and thank heaven always wake up before it arrives. Then I throw up.

I am having difficulty writing this as if I am there because I blotted it all out and only remembered it and other happenings when I was in analysis.

So in hindsight this is what happened. My uncle whenever he was on leave (this went on for at least three years) would come into my room and stroke my hair, 'Your lovely silky hair'. He would move his hands down my body and then put his huge thing against my hair and move it around my face and mouth, sometimes in my mouth, and then take out a handkerchief and turn his back on me. Then he would leave, saying how beautiful I was, reminding me to keep our secret. His voice was threatening. He was a huge man.

My door opened and shut on a latch. Eventually I put my tooth brush in it so that it couldn't be lifted, but Granny found out that I was locking my door and told me not to be a silly girl. There was nothing to be scared of. I was not to lock it.

I knew nothing, understood nothing of what he was doing, but what he did made me physically sick and scared, scared that if I didn't do what he wanted he might harm me or possibly kill me. Worst of all, there was no one looking after me. And I dared not tell.

Luckily my uncle was badly wounded at the front and was invalided out of the army – so he and his family moved to a house in Beaconsfield. Somehow I came through it all. I made myself believe it never happened. I loved looking after the animals especially the rabbits, and gave them names. Flopsy, Mopsy, Cottontail and Peter. I was told off for refusing to eat them. Sidney understood. He wouldn't kill them. They were given to our butcher in the village who knocked them on the head, skinned them and cut them into pieces for Auntie Agnes to make into a stew.

I played a lot of sport, tennis and croquet, and read book upon book upon book.

I was miserable at Pinewood, and nervous. I had head-aches and was often dizzy. I didn't understand what was going on in me, why I turned my face away if a man walked past me when I was sitting down – afraid that I might smell that smell. I no longer liked or trusted human beings, not the women because they didn't take care of me, nor the men who were dangerous. I only loved my rabbits, chickens and Pink Ears the pig, and a little bit Sidney, gentle storytelling Sidney. He told me the tale about the Princess with the Golden Hair who escaped her cruel step-parents supported by her animal friends. They went through trials and dangers together; they were always courageous, patient and kind. They finally arrived in a place of beauty and bounty – meadows and shelters for the animals and lo and behold (I loved that phrase) a handsome prince who fell in love with her, and his mother the Queen who cared for her and would brush and dress her silky hair. The Prince and the Princess married and lived happily ever after. Because it was wartime there were of course real dangers – the air raids, the flying bombs, the Messerschmitt that crashed up in the woods – but they held no fear for me. I would not have minded if I'd gone to sleep and never woken up. It was the Princess with the Golden Hair who helped me survive.

NB I of course now know that the 'thing' as I called it was my uncle's penis. I was totally ignorant of sex, and had never seen a naked boy or man. What an easy victim! However, from where I am now, I recognise that the Pine-

wood happenings, which could have been life crippling, were surmounted by excellent psychoanalysis. My therapy with Erik made me understand the enormous value of good parenting, and how endangered are those who, as I said somewhere, are left to the wolves. I realised that someone like Sidney and the author of the Princess with the Golden Hair were in loco parentis, redressing to a small degree the harm. I recognised that my sensitivity to the smell of people started there. Uncle David putrid and Sidney fresh, a little like newly cut grass. I learnt that stories and imagination are agents of healing. That caring for animals and their response helped compensate for my lack of safety and care. I could have done with a bit of the stroking and love that I and Sidney gave them. We both talked to them.

So, somehow I am able to say that I am recognisant of the value of all that traumatising stuff because it taught me that good therapy can put things to rights. Looking back at it all it helped me when working in prison as a therapist to unravel the complexity of someone being a sexual pervert or a psychologically or emotionally wounded criminal.

John, in his practical way, would say of traumatic events 'all grist to the mill' or 'learning curve.' Therefore one of those shit-time gifts!

come on sally look at some positives about your time there

I know I am often too negative. I must try to change that. Pinewood Lodge was a rich man's house and garden; we had eighteen acres which included a small nature reserve – in it were all sorts of exotic water birds as there were five lakes. We also had a squash court, a croquet lawn and tennis court all of which I used. The garden, or more correctly gardens, were lovely and well looked after, even though we were short of gardeners. There was an azalea garden, a heath and heather garden as I have already mentioned and a large kitchen garden and a fantastic herbaceous border. There was a large pine wood in which you could almost get lost and let your imagination run wild – terrible beasts, and hidden dangers. Even the grey squirrels would become evil messengers. Had they not killed their cousins the gentle and elegant red squirrels? To whom were they reporting? Great for story telling! Sidney was a good listener, and quite a critic. He told me to write them down, and one or two I wrote in verse. I gave them to him when I started to live in London.

Poor little rich girl!

Chapter Nineteen
Monk's Wall
Devon

Monk's Wall stood alone on a brow of a hill looking over the sea. There were no other houses within miles, except the lodge at the gate. A millionaire's indulgence; this house was built from the stones of a ruined monastery, and the roof was thatched. There were at least six bedrooms with their own bathrooms – not counting those in the servants' quarters. There were fields beyond the garden leading to the cliff's edge. Our bay dipped down on the left, and our bracken and gorse covered wilderness was on the right. Monk's Wall – even as I write the name I shiver – with sunken rose gardens where the water lily (Nymphaea alba) pond looked formal and serene, but was seething with skidding water boatmen and mating frogs. Then there was The Dell where the world was reserved for my sister and me, where we were able to light fires and swing and climb up the oak tree (Quercus robur), to our tree house. From there we could look out across the sea and listen to the clucking of the Rhode Island Reds as they laid their eggs.

my egg strong beautiful functional

To me the shape of an egg is the most exquisite design

in this world. Sacred in its symmetry. What a grown-up phrase – where did that come from! I'll use it in a poem.

sacred in its symmetry i said it at the same time as you

The hens' shiny feathers matched the rusty soil in the orchard behind us. One night they died petrified, turned into stuffed birds, and I saw them. The gardener said it was a fox that scared them but I wondered.

The same thing happened in the Cathedral Close in Exeter; a whole group of people having tea were killed, turned into statues, by shock from the bombing.

When we were in The Dell Gill was Susan and I was Tilly from *Swallows and Amazons*. We were happier when we were being someone else. Near our dell there was a thatched barn for apple storing, neat rows of Russets and Cox's Orange Pippins. A few were bruised and if they touched their neighbours, the gardener told us, would rot the lot. I was tempted to knock them together because it was over orderly. Once I made one shelf into a cider smelling mass with wasps on top. The gardener put a lock, a padlock on the oak barn door. The apple barn had a sophisticated sister – we could tell that all the buildings were related because they all had grey heavily thatched roofs. This one was called the summer house but no sun got in it, for like all the buildings on the estate the windows were small, the walls thick and the thatch sloped almost down to the ground. We used to slide down the thatch on the side away from the house and from the darkness of its interior we looked out to the wide bright sea. The contrast of the light and gloom was so fierce it cut. It was in this summer house that the local cubs and scouts would meet. Gill and I enjoyed their company when we could join in. My uncle was a great supporter of the scouting movement, and the boys were often asked into the house for tea.

Often and often over the ups and downs of the beautifully manicured lawns I would run to a horseshoe shaped platform enclosed by grassy banks except on the side with the view of the sea. This was my very own place away from the house, and I opened my arms toward the sea. Asking or accepting what I did not know.

gestures will do not knowing will do

Then there was the tennis court with another small thatched relation as a shelter, and it was here that I started to love the game. There was the cob nut walk to reach it – they are still my favourite nuts.

In the Spring the orchards were yellow and white with daffodils and narcissi, and there was the crab apple tree (Malus sylvestris) whose bright red apples belied their taste, bitter but beautiful like the one offered Snow White by the wicked witch – my great aunt who with my great uncle owned Monk's Wall. Aunt Lily loved my sister who had been there from when she first went to the boarding school at Woodside House.

She never liked me. Uncle Anthony was a millionaire who collected houses and things and somehow Gill and I had been added to his collection. This had been agreed by our guardians Aunt Elinor on my mother's side and Granny on my father's, for he was at war. Gill and I were now Wards of Court. We got letters from our father and sometimes from Mummy, whom I only saw twice more in my life as she lived in Scotland where she was married to my godfather, a Scottish laird. I wished I was with her in Scotland.

The great uncle and great aunt always took walking

sticks when they went out, and sliced the tops off the delicately poised Spring flowers and swiped at Bill, the placid Labrador, but mostly at the plants. My uncle, Uncle Anthony, had weak eyes and we decided he needed a stick to beat out his revenge. It was because the light hurt his eyes that the house was dark with tiny windows, the walls thick, made of red rocks not stones, brought to this house from the old ruined medieval monastery up on our wilderness where we would go for picnics; the air was sea blown, clear and bright.

We never talked of the fear built into the house, but we knew it. It was luxurious, large wood fires burning, deep Persian carpets, and down filled armchairs and sofas. There were beautiful paintings and bronze statues of lovely looking boys, many of them naked, and ancient firing pistols and Elizabethan pitch forks. Gill and I decided to use them against the German invaders, and we each kept a pot of pepper under our bed to blind them when they landed with their parachutes.

There was a servants' quarters behind green baize doors where we both went to feel happy with Cook and Etta the maid. We helped make cakes, and Etta and Mrs Coomber always hugged us and made us laugh.

My bedroom was next door to the one where my sister slept with Aunt Lily. We called her Auntie Blossom, or Bloss for short, but she did not know it. My bathroom had antique Dutch tiles, my bedroom central heating under the window seat; this is where I would sit and look out at the light and the sea. Uncle Anthony had what was called black market connections, so that is why we had fuel for the boilers, and butter and cream because he owned a nearby farm.

I would shiver when I went into the other rooms thinking I might see something I didn't want to see, something that was enclosed in that house. The feeling was so strong that I would rush out to where the old monastery used to be and standing on a broken wall would cleanse myself in the wind, and ask for deliverance – deliver us from evil – for Gill and me from that dark house, and the crying gulls.

i heard you and comforted you

And then I felt better.

We would take our swimming things down to the bay, the red cove, and we would swim way out and let the sea water wash our fears away, then we would walk slowly up the hill tired from swimming out too far and not wanting to return to the house.

Sometimes in the evening I would walk out on the terrace and look up at the sky, at the stars and the moon and the white scudding clouds, and say take me, take me away, lift me out of this,

you'd stand on tiptoe and stretch your arms up towards the sky seeking me

Some days while we waited, when the wind was blowing strongly from the sea, we would wear our strong navy blue raincoats and walk to the cliff at the high part near the ruined monastery, and undoing our buttons we would open out our macs, holding them wide like wings and lean out over the cliff's edge against the wind. We did not mind if we lived or died. Gill and I never talked of our fear and grief.

the wind never failed you

Afterwards we would hold a service in the crumbled monastery all praise and singing and dancing.

you wondered if the ground was still holy from those old days
and if any of your silent prayers would be answered
i always answer in my own way

I started to write poems at this time. I longed for my mother to come and rescue me.

I was abandoned by her and I had to let her die even if only in a poem. I didn't keep them but put them in bottles and threw them out to sea.

NB At Monk's Wall fear came into my life in big way; an unfocused fear. Fear for my sister sleeping in the same room as Aunt Lily. Perhaps somewhere deep down where I had hidden it, I remembered how frightened but happy I had been in my mother's bed.

Fear of some unknown thing that was going on between my uncle and the cubs. Fear that some people were capable of causing other people to die of fright while they were gently taking tea. If someone could swipe the heads off beautiful plants just for the hell of it what else might they do?

I could sense danger and was glad to have Gill there to protect me from what I did not know. And I was there for her. I was a tough strong tom-boy, and I've just recalled, always carried a pocket knife. We were dressed in grey shorts just like the cubs, who really enjoyed our play room with the ping-pong table and games, and scrumptious Devon teas – scones, which we sometimes helped Cook make, strawberry jam and clotted cream. I noticed that some of the cubs were nervous, as I so often felt.

Alongside all of this Gill and I had the certainty that the wind was looking after us, and that the fresh air and the

*sea were cleaning us. We would play and dance and sing,
for whom we did not know or care, but we knew there was
an appreciative audience.*

a ha

*Those were the times when we were happy. Of course I now
know that my uncle was homosexual, in fact he was also
a paedophile but he was never reported. Too well known
and rich. When I was about twenty I and Tim, a boyfriend,
went swimming in the pool in his Surrey home and he tried
to seduce him. It didn't worry me, as by then I knew about
sex. It just annoyed me.*

*Later I remembered one of the poems I wrote when we
were in Devon, or at least its content. It was simpler and
less worked and rubbed and polished than this one, which
is included in Break Through, a collection of my poems.
I think the original might have been the better one, and
wonder if it is still floating about somewhere.*

*Most of my poems arrive complete. It is as if someone else
is writing inside me.*

me

*Like when I typed that phrase 'sacred symmetry'. Where
did it come from?*

me

*I am a child and stand above the grave,
in it is a coffin wrought by me,
worked and rubbed and polished
until the sun's reflection
is almost as bright as the sun.*

My head nodding slowly
accepting a great decision.

Beyond the grave,
over the cliff's edge is the sea,
it's even flow and retreat
meeting me,
and the cry of the gulls.
I can hear the shingle being sucked away,
feel myself slipping with the undertow,
being dragged under by the Coelacanth [As a child I must have looked
up sea monsters in the encyclopaedia; I know Coelacanth
was in the original.]
waiting in dark seaweed forests
below the pulse of the sea.

song

So I put the earth
On the lid of the box
With my wooden spade
And began to enjoy
The pitch and the toss
Filling the hole that I made

I began to destroy
The grief and the loss
And danced on the grave

Chapter Twenty
My Hut
Willow Cabin

I don't know how other poets find their poems but this is how I do. By the time a poem arrives in written form it is complete. It comes hand written, says what I want in the way that I want, and if I'm not entirely happy with it, there is little to be done. Although it comes entire it can take months, sometimes years to make. It happens out of sight, inside my body.

I'll try to explain.

When I was a child and hadn't acquired the words for things and feelings I packed them – the words and the feelings that hadn't words – away in cellars, store rooms, cupboards and attics in my body – things I found too precious to be shown the light of day, or too frightening to be shared with uncomprehending adults; like the sensual delight I experienced while jogging on their unsuspecting knees. 'This is the way the ladies ride trit trot trit trot' (titillating) 'This is the way the gentlemen ride canter, canter, canter' (more interesting) 'This is the way the farmers ride gerumph, gerumph, gerumph' (rough and really exciting) Definitely to be locked in the cellar to which only I had the key.

Or later in primary school when we sang the exquisite round written in a minor key. 'Ah, poor bird, take thy

flight Far above the sorrows of this sad night.' The pain
I shared with the bird was too strong for decency. I knew
that sad black night; the words seemed holy, for 'thy' is a
god's pronoun.

I made the song fly up into the attic.

My heavy drinking father told me the two most beautiful words in the English language were 'cellar door'. He
had wanted me baptised Cellardoor instead of Sarah.

Then there were the ringing sounds from the bible.
'Behold the lilies of the field.'

'Comfort thyself what comfort is in me.' All feeding the religious fervour that I felt for something. These
phrases had to be caught and rescued from the ordinary
school chapel and be put away in a most privileged part
of my body.

And experiences that were too sweet, too exciting, too
sharp, were wrapped up, even if I had at the time no
words for them, and stored securely away.

When I was a little older I started to enjoy reading,
especially poetry, and as I read it out loud I was able to
identify physically with the material, and the experiences
of others. Gratefully, consciously and carefully I put these
on the shelves in my store rooms. Luckily there was lots
of space.

'But yet the pity of it. Iago! O! Iago the pity of it.'
This encompassed all disaster and it nestled down slightly
uncomfortably next to 'It was, you might say satisfactory'.

'Beaded bubbles winking at the brim' made love to
'happy as the grass was green'. Phrase upon phrase jostled
for position and settled on their shelves. Ecstasy flew up to
the eaves –

'When I behold upon the night's starred face
Huge cloudy symbols of a high romance'

Then down to the cellar in despair went 'Pitched past

pitch of grief' and found its equilibrium by meeting laughter, ''Twas brillig and the slithy toves'.

Words, sense, nonsense, rhyme, music, symbols, love, boredom, fun and hurt met in the corridors and responded and reacted to one another.

And sometimes, on such and such a day something happens outside this body of mine, a 'now' happening, and if the conditions are right out through a tiny concentrated aperture in my body comes a poem with all its fingers and toes, and when I read it out loud I might say 'its nose reminds me just a bit of Grandpa Solomon, its shape is just a little reminiscent of cousin John, its appetites like Dylan's, and maybe there's the slightest touch of Emily...'

But in spite of its inheritance it is itself.

Chapter Twenty-One
Woodside House School

While I was living at Monk's Wall I was at boarding school in Budleigh Salterton, the same one that Gill had been to. We were once again separated as she was now at her public school in Surrey. My uniform, which had been Gill's, was a lovely cornflower blue, (Centaurea cyanus) and I loved it partly because of the bright colour after my boring grey one, and partly because Gill had worn it.

I enjoyed school as I was really good at everything except arithmetic and I wasn't bad at that. I loved learning Latin properly, not just out of our flower book, and French. I remember the word for the sea was la mer, almost the same as the word for mother, la mere, and wondered if that is why I loved looking at and swimming in the sea. Perhaps I thought of that when I was older, but I was, as they said in my school report, precocious. I do remember looking up the word, and feeling proud that I was precocious.

I was good at sport, rounders and tennis. One day when we were playing rounders, not the time when I hit the ball, you know they're pretty hard, and by mistake hit Joy who was laughing, in the mouth and broke her front teeth – this was another time. There was the sound of ack ack fire; we saw the puffs of smoke and a plane coming towards us.

'Run, run into the gym, hurry girls!' But I stayed where I was as I remembered my father saying 'Lie flat, then you are not so much of a target'. The plane came right down, a machine gun firing and I saw the young man's face, he was that close. These were called sneak raids. He then went down the road to the grammar school but couldn't get at them because they had a school yard with high walls, not a playing field. I wasn't frightened of the bullets but I wish I hadn't seen his face. I was ticked off for not obeying the games teacher. I wondered who to believe, who to listen to, obey? It made me very very sad that that man would want to kill me and those other children, I was also red hot angry.

The headmistress was a super teacher, Latin and English were her subjects, all the words, poetry, and stories were alive, bouncing off the pages of the books, and she kept rabbits. Not ordinary ones, Rexes. There were Lilac, Havana, and Sable Rexes, and she chose me to help look after them. Miss Gregory, we called her G G or sometimes Horse, but she didn't know it, only wore a skirt for teaching, the rest of the time she wore jodhpurs. The rabbits had lots of babies, and they were cuddly, beautiful and sweet. I felt lucky and worked hard at keeping all the hutches clean with fresh sawdust.

We had an outside gym and I liked to go there and climb the bars, and hang upside down, 'You are old Father William', like him it gave me a different view of the world.

I used to climb the ropes and had a lovely feeling as I slid down, the rope between my legs.

Most nights we could hear the German planes coming over on their way to bomb Exeter. We could tell how many had been shot down by the change of engine noise when they came back. In my last term I was head of dorm, and one night I seemed to be doing something wrong, I think

I was eating Ovaltine tablets under the bed clothes. G G came in and caught me and told me to go with her. She took me to her bedroom, a panelled room with a large four poster bed. She said she was going to cane me, and told me to bend over the arm of an armchair. She pulled down my pyjama trousers and stroked me, and then hit me six times saying things that I didn't understand because she was really hurting me. She was in her night things. She spent some time looking at me before telling me to dress. 'Sarah, don't show anyone your red marks, or tell them you were caned. This is just between you and me, because you are a naughty, naughty girl, but you were brave and didn't cry.' Then she ruffled my hair. I was sore, but proud of myself and I felt like a courageous boy and in a way I had quite enjoyed it, it made me feel special, and I had a secret.

At Speech Day at the end of that Summer term I was awarded the Record Cup and GG made it clear how much I deserved it. I knew I had done well at work and sport, but I was not really the best pupil, and I secretly felt ashamed. I knew it was because I was her favourite.

Looking back at that time I had such a mixture of feelings; exciting lessons, strange sensations, lovely rabbits and the thrill of sport; but again the feeling that I wasn't safe, and I was dangerously alone. It wasn't the Germans I was frightened of, it was something else.

I was meant to go back to Woodside House for one more term, but it was closed down as Miss Gregory was not well and had been told she could no longer teach.

A convent school took over and the uniform was brown. I still had my blue uniform as it was only for one term. There was no-one else from the old school and I felt an outsider, and did not like their prayers. I was the only girl who was not a Roman Catholic, and I wouldn't cross myself or genuflect.

I loved the trees, the sky, the sea, and told them so. 'I love you clouds.'

thank you

I spent most of the term alone and didn't make a friend. Why was I left in this awful school? Why wasn't it checked out? I had no-one to talk to about how unhappy I was. I was trying to be brave as I didn't want anyone to think badly of my family, not even me.

Then there was the dentist – I had to go five times, and each time I was on my own. He had a foreign accent and I thought he might kill me with his jars of coloured liquids, and his terrible drill. I needed Gill or some grown-up to protect me. I was hurt and frightened.

Brown uniform, brown Catholics, brown lessons: a dark brown time.

NB What have I gleaned from this time? I notice that there is only one remark in italics. It seems that a religious school is not very conducive to god talk. I imagine G G was removed from Woodside House because she was considered morally unfit to be in charge of young girls. You could say she was unwell. Someone must have reported her.

I missed the wonderful lessons, the rabbits and my friends. I missed G G, especially her enthusiasm for Latin and the way she pointed out to us the origin of many of our English words. For example, instead of 'reported her' I could have put 'someone must have denounced her.' That was a word I learnt in Latin class. 'Nuntius messenger denouncer.' I remember some others: 'Credere accept as true miscreant' 'Dormire to sleep dormitory' 'Sarah don't interrupt.' 'Rumpere to burst or break interrupt.'

I just loved understanding how the words came into being. Words and the English language were becoming a passion. In my report from the brown school (that I think was called St Therese) it was stated that 'Sarah is taciturn'. Tacre to be silent taciturn.

I was beginning to suppress my joy in learning, participating, curiosity. I was closing down.

Chapter Twenty-Two
Nayland Place

It was a small dark cottage with dilapidated furniture, but cosy. There was no central heating because fuel was rationed, as were our food and clothes. Auntie Nen was sweet to us and we had wood fires and not bad meals. I slept in Mummy's room in a single bed beside her double one.

I went to a weekly boarding school in Colchester which I did not like and our uniform was grey. We had to do one lesson a day wearing gas masks, and I thought I might stop breathing. At night I slept in a dormitory with five other girls, or was meant to sleep but was awake most of the night as I had bad dreams of weird monsters that I almost recognised, and they were after me. But the weekends were lovely. Auntie Nen taught Mummy and me how to knit, and we made socks and wristlets for the soldiers at the front. We also made up shows for the men in the hospital. Mummy played the piano and had a beautiful deep singing voice, and I sang too. We did 'Run Rabbit', 'The White Cliffs of Dover' and on my own I danced and sang 'Somewhere Over The Rainbow'. Mummy was very good at 'Lili Marlene'. As she was the quartermaster for the hospital, we sang 'The Quartermaster's Store' and I was the snakes and the rats. It was great.

I love the smell of bread cooking and whenever I could I helped the hospital's baker, sometimes kneading the dough with him. Mummy and I used to take the provisions, as they were called, to the hospital by pony and trap, which I drove. Star was the pony's name as she had a white star between her ears. I was so happy doing all these things with Mummy.

I went to bed a long time before her, and I used to pretend to be asleep when she came up. She was different at night. She would come into the room, wobbly. I think she was very very tired. Sometimes she'd talk to herself and sometimes cry, 'Bill. Bill', Daddy's name, and once 'Why have you deserted me?' She was often drinking something from our tooth mug, or would make some cocoa on our gas burner, and sometimes she would fall asleep without putting on her nightie. Many nights I would get into bed with her, as I wanted to make her better and we would cuddle.

Difficult things started happening. First of all some of Auntie Nen's jewellery went missing, and my watch on the red strap vanished. When I was looking for it in our chest of drawers I found some bottles underneath her jerseys and some bills for quite a lot of money, but I never found my watch, which made me sad as it was my first grown-up present. I didn't tell anyone about my watch or what I'd found. I kept all this to myself because I loved her so much and didn't want her to get into trouble. Something felt wrong.

One day I was shelling peas in the garden for lunch and had just removed a maggot from a pod when a car drove up. It was a big fast car, and a man and a woman got out. Aunt Elinor and Auntie Nen were there and had my green suitcase with them. 'This is Sally,' they said, and turning to me, 'You are going in the car with them, they are driving you to your grandmother.' I can only just remember what happened next. I know I spilled the peas and ran indoors to find my mother, but she was nowhere.I heard them say, 'Sally's life is endangered. There could be an accident with the boiling milk. She sleeps in her mother's bed. This is for the best. We'll send on the rest of her clothes and belongings by train.' And I remembered hearing Auntie Nen on the phone early that morning saying to Aunt Elinor something about blood, and she hoped no-one but she had seen it.

The big woman came and took my hand. 'Come along Sally, be a good girl now. As your Auntie says, this is for the best. Come on, dear!'

I can't remember what happened next. Did anyone hug me, did we say goodbye?

I felt nothing, nothing. I can remember nothing, nothing, nothing. Not even Mummy.

NB Of course I now understand what was going on, and that it was necessary to move me from harm's way but it should have been done differently: I was quite old enough to be talked to and confided in. The aunts should have told me that Mummy had a drink problem and was ill (I already knew having found those whisky bottles) and that she had agreed – even if it wasn't true – that I should go to my Grandmother. I do realise they couldn't tell me of her attempted suicide. Perhaps one of them should have accompanied me. That police car made me feel frightened. I didn't like their smell. I temporarily switched off, cut off my feelings and went cold. This opting out became a strategy of mine, a truly detrimental one that can and did lead to psychosomatic illnesses.

How I enjoyed the times when Mummy and I sang and performed for the troops, our pony trap journeys and knitting. Our war effort! I loved being in bed with her and cud-

dling. Why the aunts thought there was anything untoward going on was their problem. I buried all those happy memories away along with the painful ones, but now as I am writing this I am filled with warm feelings of love for my mother.

It was just after this that Gill and I were made Wards of Court. The two guardians were our father's mother and Aunt Elinor on our mother's side.

Looking back at my rupture from my mother I now know that it was the worst happening in my life. I refused to acknowledge it, recognise it. It was too unbearable. I wasn't there. It didn't happen. I switched off.

Chapter Twenty-Three
Tanglewood

We only had a short time here. Just the three of us. Mummy, Gill and me. I am surprised at how happy I felt. I was on a great adventure with my big sister and we had our mother to ourselves; we wanted to make her happy. We knew she missed her life in London, our servants, Nanny, and Daddy.

It was holiday time so we had no school work. We hardly thought about the past, although I remember thinking how much the Scotties would have loved being in the country. I really missed them. We went for walks in the huge cemetery which was just nearby. It was full of dead people, gravestones and flowers, and there was a stream with bulrushes (Typha latifolia) and sun-bright shiny flowers called kingcups (Caltha palustris), sometimes known as marsh marigolds, or water blobs. We found a book on plants in the study and we began to know which plant was which, and learnt their names. I loved it that each one had at least two names, always one in Latin. I never knew which name I enjoyed saying the most, so I used them all depending on how I felt and invented some myself, sun blob for instance.

Mummy never came out with us as she was very very tired. It worried her that she did not know how to cook, not even a boiled egg, although she tried. She told us she had never washed or ironed clothes in all her life, but we all enjoyed learning how. One of the things thing that helped us, because the village shop was too far for us to walk to and then carry everything back, was that they delivered all we ordered. An old man called Mr Price would come twice a week riding his bike, with our food and some clanking bottles in the small cart which he towed behind him.

Something was wrong with our mother; she slept a lot, and hardly ate at all.

We mostly ate picnic meals which Gill and I really liked. Mummy said she was discouraged and stopped trying to cook altogether and mostly stayed in bed.

It was decided by my grandmother and the local doctor that my mother couldn't cope and a new plan was made. She and I would go to live near to her Aunt Elinor, called Auntie Frog in secret by Gill and me because she looked like one, who was a famous doctor and surgeon in charge of a big hospital for wounded soldiers. We, Mummy and I, were to live nearby with another friend called Auntie Nen, who had a spare room, and the two aunts would look after us.

Gill they said was now big enough to go to a boarding school in Devon, which was near to where another great aunt lived, and a safe part of England.

We went for a goodbye walk in the cemetery, and I picked her a bunch of the brightest blue water forget-me-nots (Myosotis scorpioides).

So that is what happened.

NB We never did forget each other although we were very seldom together. It was awful being without Gill, but worse for her; at least I had our mother.

I notice there are no remarks in italics. Maybe I was just not tuned in. It struck me even at that age, how apposite it was that we said goodbye surrounded by tombstones remembering the dead. Significant would be a better word than apposite. All those losses, one small death after another. Our London home and school, Hunky and Fussy the Scotties, Fraulein, Nanny, Daddy, our dancing class, the lamp lighters, the round pond and feeding the ducks; all that was familiar.

But the greatest loss of all, my sister.

Chapter Twenty-Four
Onslow Gardens

Our school uniform is purple – but some of it is grey. We are old enough now to dress ourselves. After breakfast we always go to Mummy's bedroom to say goodbye. She is drinking fizzy water. We kiss her and she says goodbye to us, and be good.

Our school is near to where we live in Onslow Gardens, so either Nanny or Fraulein walks with us. I love school, specially reading and writing stories, poems and painting. The best day of the week is Thursday when I go to Madame Vincent's dancing class. I have a small green suitcase with my ballet shoes, tunic and skipping rope. A fat smiley lady plays the piano and we start by skipping and I finish by flitting my wings and turning into a butterfly. I have to wait for Gill who is in a class for older girls. She is learning to be a shooting star, and will dance on her own in the show we are doing at a huge theatre called The Scala. I and my class are the Milky Way. Last year Gill was a violet and I was a daisy. Mummy's dressmaker makes lovely costumes for us. We go to lots of birthday parties and I have a blue velvet cloak and am careful not to walk on the lines because of the bears. I love coming home because the lights are lit and it is a new sort of world. I often watch the man lighting the lamps from our bedroom window. Of course I am talking about winter time. Once we had snow and we had another new sort of world. And Christmas is a special time. We get a big present that Gill and I share. One year we had a shop you could walk into, another time a doll's house that had proper lights in it. We put pillow cases at the foot of our beds for Father Christmas to fill – I don't believe in him but pretend to for the grown-ups' sake. That Father Christmas at Harrods had makeup on his face, and he was a different one when I went a second time with my best friend Rachel. One year we went to 'Peter Pan' and I was the only one who shouted NO when Tinkerbell asked if we believed in fairies. I got so many bad looks, tutting noises, and Gill poked me, that perhaps it is better to pretend I do. I love the idea of the Flower Fairies, my favourite book, and Tinkerbell, but they are just ideas made to look real.

Sometimes I can tell my thoughts to Gill, but not so often as when I was small.

More often I talk to someone or something in myself, or very close to me.

that s me

One Christmas, after we had the pudding – I got two charms and Gill a sixpence – something horrid happened. Mummy and Daddy and two of their friends, Auntie Jan and Uncle Philip, were laughing loudly (we called all their friends Aunt and Uncle even though they weren't), drinking lots and telling funny stories, when Mummy knocked over a candle. The cotton wool snow caught fire, and flames shot up. We got down without asking and ran away from the table. Daddy put it out with the water from Gill's and my water jug. He told us to come back to the table as it was cracker time. We all put on our paper hats and

Auntie Jan read out 'Why did the chicken cross the road?' We didn't know the answer. 'In order to get to the other side'. Gill and I laughed because it was quite funny, but we didn't feel like it, and asked if we could get down. We held hands as we went to our nursery, for something bad had happened in the dining-room.

In the summers we spent a lot of time in our house in Ferring. It had a ha-ha at the bottom of the garden so it looked like the beach was ours. We had a hut on the beach where we kept our bathing things and spades and games. Mummy and Daddy sometimes came down from London with their friends, and had parties on the beach and in the garden. Fraulein was often at the parties as she was pretty, but not Nanny. Mummy and Daddy liked to have holidays abroad in places like – Oh, I can't remember. I hated seeing their suitcases in the hall; I thought they wouldn't come back.

One evening in London we were in the drawing room to say goodnight and four of their friends were there. Each evening we could always take three almonds from a little silver plate. Mummy, Daddy and their friends did not seem happy and had black voices, and they did not stop talking as we came in. About Germany, soldiers in boots goose-stepping, someone called Chamberlain, and Adolph Hitler. Mummy said 'Darlings, take your almonds up to bed, and kiss us all goodnight'. Everyone hugged us in very special way.

A few days later I heard Daddy speaking in an angry voice to Fraulein. 'You are to leave immediately. Go back to Germany and your Fuhrer. Here is your month's pay and a train ticket.' Gill and I were very sad to see her leave and I gave Fraulein my book called *The Flower Fairies*. Mummy, Gilly, Fraulein and I cried.

This was the start of everyone leaving because London

was going to be a dangerous place to live. There was a wailing sound that went up and down and made me scared 'Sally, it's only a siren – they are trying it out. It will warn us to take shelter.' 'Why?' 'Because the Germans are going to bomb us.' And then a long smooth wail. 'That is called the All Clear. It's only a practice.' It is the siren that frightens me – a terrible sick sound, a sound like badness. I'm glad we're packing up our things.

Daddy was the first to go because when he was young he was a soldier. He was a major and went off to fight the Germans. Then Hunky and Fussy our Scotties went to a nice safe home. Nanny went to Wales to look after her mother, Cook and the maids left, and the butler was called up and became a soldier. All our furniture and our toys went to be kept in Granny's squash court in the garden of her home in Windlesham, and Sidney, Granny's chauffeur, came to fetch us in the Rolls.

I had my green suitcase, and Teddy was inside it. Gill and I said 'good-bye house.'

Mummy shut our red front door behind us.

NB Am I already suspecting that some things are lies, and am I beginning to realise that in order to belong I needed to lie too? Do we lose God when we lose our truth? I notice that here there are no italics except that very faint 'that's me.' I did not believe in Santa Claus or fairies. I did not believe Germans were bad, or that my father had the right to kill them. I had loved Fraulein and was starting not to give credence to my feelings and beliefs. Maybe that is why there were so few italic sentences. It was not a happy Christmas dinner, yet we were meant to laugh. They weren't happy, but acted so. My mother was out of control and dangerous. I knew it, but she was my mother so I let myself be deluded. Was it safer that way? I now think the Scotties never went to their safe and loving home but were put down. How easily the young are perverted from the truth! I couldn't tell anyone except Gill how much I missed Nanny, Fraulein, Cook and the butler. Gill told me of the expression 'stiff upper lip'. It is true that one's top lip quivers when you start to cry. Although it was the school holidays it really upset us both to realise that we wouldn't be going back to our school or to our dancing class. The school moved out to Kent, away from town and miles away from Granny's. Looking back on the whole upheaval of leaving London I realise that Mummy was pre-occupied, drinking too much, and forgot about us.

Chapter Twenty-Five
Onslow Gardens

'in my beginning is my end' T S Eliot

Nanny! Ow, the soap's in my eye – look how me in the mirror looks at me in that other mirror that looks at me in this one – just goes on and on and...

infinity infinity

I know, I know. I've just found out.

Nanny, you're washing me too hard! I won't say that prayer Gill and me have to say each night – anyway not the part that says please to someone make me a good girl – I am one. 'Please God, make me a good girl.'

no need you are one i know i know

'Nanny, Granny, Mummy, Daddy, Gill and all my kind friends and relations.'

I am meant to ask God, when I think they mean me

there is no difference i know i know

to bless them. What's that mean? Be good, be good to

them?

just be you are i know i know.

Nanny, leave Gill and me alone. Stop telling us. Gilly says, and she is seven, that we want to have our own thoughts. We don't like saying your prayers.

you have no need to

I think I'm lovely and so is Gilly.

yes

Sometimes a bit bossy, but she is almost three years older than me. And Teddy, by the way not bossy – lovely. And hot chocolate, and Hunky and Fussy (short for Behunkus and Josephus) our Scotty dogs. If they make me say that prayer I'll say the words out loud, but there'll be no me behind it. I and Gilly have not met God, have not been introduced. Would we curtsy like we have been taught when we meet new grown-ups? Or is God a child like me?

quite so no need to bob
   you can't meet me because you and i are one you have my permission to drop my name i don't need to be named to exist
we know we do yes yes

I want to hug you, and Gilly, Mummy and Daddy, because I love you – and just a little bit you Nanny.
   Now Gill and I are in our dressing gowns and Nanny is taking us down to the big drawing room where Mummy and Daddy are having their evening drink. We often don't get a chance to hug them, but we are always allowed three

nuts. Daddy says they are called almonds, and they ask as they always do if we have been good today. Yes, yes, we say. We say goodnight and I go to kiss Mummy but she turns away. It doesn't feel good not hugging Mummy, so I'll hug Teddy when I get into bed.

On the way upstairs Gilly sees I'm crying and says Mummy couldn't hug us as she is in her party dress, and doesn't want it crumpled. They are having friends to dinner. We take off our dressing gowns and hang them on the two hooks marked Sarah and Gill. No prayers tonight as it is Nanny's evening off. She is in her room changing out of her uniform, and we guess putting on some lipstick. She calls out, 'Gill and Sarah turn out your bedside lights!' But we already have.

a white light is all around you

I love my bed, with Gilly in the bed next to me, and cuddling Teddy. I dream and dream. I dream of coming from a bright and beautiful place and coming to this bright and beautiful place and I am happy.

benedicte

NB Well, I made it! Almost back to my birth. I couldn't go right back because my memory doesn't stretch that far. I feel released, as if I have transcended many of the conformations and assumptions that stopped me from knowing. Knowing what? That my life is my meaning, that those 'italic thoughts' came from me/God, that love is non judgemental, all embracing, that those people that I met, some of whom I am still meeting, are wonderful in its true sense; the prisoners, Samuel, John, my children, Gill. By the way I still am in touch with one of the tearaway boys. He is an electrician and his brothers and sisters are doing OK. He tells me his mother who is now married is going to ask me to tea. More tea!

I am so glad to have relived those WOW moments – hints of the divine, that are now so obvious and are still resonating today. That egg, that divine egg! The language it inspired, sacred symmetry, pretty sophisticated for a twelve year old. I now know where it came from, and realise I was being inspired to become a poet. The dead people I have loved and I still love are alive in me. Well done Dylan, 'death shall have no dominion'. I know that not knowing many things is exhilarating and freeing. The last episode when I was only four years old was the final clarification. Then I just got on with it, lived in the present, truthfully and simply. I just was. I expressed my feelings and was not judgemental or analytical. To my disadvantage I learned that later! At that time I, a solid little being, was my spirit. My spirit was embodied and in tune with living.

I felt safe and loved, and loved my Teddy and my sister. I still have the bear, worn through to the straw, and wearing the green pullover that I made at Nayland House when my mother and I knitted, chaotically but determinedly, for the troops.

When I first began writing my story, starting from when I was sixty-nine and taking you back to when I was very young, I wasn't sure it was the best method of sorting myself out, or whether I'd find my life had meaning and whether I'd find there is a god, a spiritual dimension to the universe and my being, and that all experience has relevance. I hoped to be sure that I would decide to stay alive and live my life out until my god appointed death, and that old-age-life would be worth living.

I was surprised that I was as present when writing about the distant past as I was in the years just lived. The whole *process made clear my understanding of time, and that the past is the present; and as for the future it does not exist – simply because it hasn't been! My angst has evaporated. With no more fear about a future that isn't, I have more energy: I feel quite bubbly; the depression is gone. The process of really re-experiencing events in my life confirmed my way of working as a therapist; that by reliving certain events, risking the feelings they evoke and expressing them, proves the value of the experience, even a shitty one, and then you can accept how essential it was in your evolving. By making it known to have been necessary to your development it puts the event into its place. The ghosts are laid.*

For me the Uncle David horror story was nearly paralysing to recollect, but getting it out and writing it down was far more efficacious than revealing it in my analysis. As I was quiet and alone when writing I was focused on the remembering and was not censoring myself and the story for the sake of protecting Erik, myself and surprisingly my uncle.

Do you realise, and I am sure you do, that my uncle, my great uncle and G G my headmistress would now if they had been reported – be sentenced as paedophiles? I must add that I do not think their acts were criminal, but sick and harmful and that prison for the likes of them is not the right place. They should be put in a secure environment, out of harming way; and given treatment. The perpetrators should be asked to name their victims and they should be given therapy too. Many of the injured, and I choose the word carefully, feel too ashamed or frightened to admit to the abuse, often believing they had in some way invited it. I think that was the reason I had thought to become a prostitute. I considered myself to be one already.

Thank you readers for being there. I feel safe in your heads, and you have helped me. I have let you know what

I would have once thought should be kept secret, and only good has come of it.

So I could now say that the meaning of my life is living and through living God in me is incarnate; something like that! Perhaps better to say the meaning of my life is life. I have found the god I needed to find or to put it another way I know God (the word I was no longer going to use but can't find another). I know this through a non physical sense that is wordless, and thus I cannot name.

thank the lord

Why am I smiling? Did I hear something?

My life that I had thought to end has become in every conceivable way worth continuing. It is an adventure. It is a story, an illuminating story. I like it.

I like the way it has helped me understand.

I wonder, what will happen next?

I need to spend some time reflecting, so I will open the Willow Cabin's door – it is a lovely red one, the same colour as our front door in Onslow Gardens, and go in.

Chapter Twenty-Six
The Hut
Willow Cabin

Tennis Croquet Getting in the flow

I had thought that my last reflections in the Willow Cabin would be profound, on subjects such as truth, spirituality, well being, but O no, tennis and croquet have imposed themselves. They say they are equally important. They advocate play, fun, and skill.

I have come into the hut still wearing whites. It is compulsory on the front lawns when playing croquet. I'll write about croquet in a little while. Just now I want to think about tennis, the beautiful game. This will be bit of a requiem, maybe a post mortem, for having broken my ankle in two places I no longer play. However, at the time of the accident, which was quite recent, I was inspired to write a short play based on the incident. Its title is 'Break a Leg'. In it I look at matters close to some of the conclusions I have reached in my life; that events that seem catastrophic can become an opportunity, a time to take stock, look inward, and face the truth about oneself; that one can accept the need to change and do so often with a helper, who in the play is a character called Alfie, and find the meaning in all that life throws at one, and recognise God wherever and however she/he manifests herself/

himself. Here is an extract from it. No, not an extract. I have decided to put the whole play in (it is a short one) as it complements this story of mine. It touches on old age, the ability to change and to accept the help that is given.

I have temporarily left the Willow Cabin, but will return after you have read and I hope enjoyed 'Break a Leg'.

Chapter Twenty-Seven
BREAK A LEG
by Sarah Benson

Dramatis Personae

(ages are guidelines, except for Laura and Catherine)

Laura   74 A patient. Aspiring writer. At the start
                she is superior, hard, angry and critical.
                She comes to terms with many of her
                problems during her time in hospital.
                In fact she changes quite significantly
                with help from Alfie and the people she
                encounters. No great voice, but can sing.

Alfie   45 Strong Cockney accent. A mix of
                Michael Caine and God. A great sense
                of fun, loving and profound. A showman.
                Plays the mouth organ very well. *(a musi-
                cian could play the off stage music)*

Actor(s)   35 Surgeon.
                25 Nurse 1. Irish.
                45 Tone, Doreen's son. Midland or
                country accent.

Actress(es)	85 Doreen. A patient. Midland or country accent.
	45 Charmian. Doreen's daughter. Midland or country accent.
	90 Catherine. A patient with Alzheimer's. Has a lovely singing voice.
	25 Nurse 2. Eastern European.
On the text.	The word 'beat' signifies a change of thought or feeling, not necessarily a pause.

Laura, Alfie and the surgeon are seen as real on stage. The other characters are in shadow/silhouette; dressed as 'women', 'men'. They are VOICES.

Laura is addicted to rhyme, thinking she is a bit of a poet, and as it becomes obvious by the end of the play that it is she who is writing this episode in her life there are many rhymes. She and Alfie enjoy and emphasise (dumpty-dum) them when they occur. The rhymes are underlined.

The music is played on a mouth organ – Alfie's instrument of choice.

in the centre taking up most of the stage there is a hospital cubicle curtained on all four sides on either side two smaller cubicles beds are indicated, not fully lit just silhouettes
   front cubicle curtain depicts scene of a tennis court

Laura	*(in tennis gear, enthusiastically)* Game. Set. Match. I love to play tennis – the bee-yooo-tiful game.

Alfie's mouth organ music

Laura   *(to audience)* What a thing to happen!
How insulting! Jumping for a volley I hit
the ball cross-court, out of reach. I win
the point but twisting lose my balance.
(falls to ground)
Crack! Crack! Oh Christ!
I'm broken. My right leg's fractured
twice.
Fibula and Tibia I shout.
That foot just there, right-angled, stick-
ing out.
The pain in everything's too dire for me
to talk about. (pause)
The crew arrive and hand me gas. (deep
breaths.)
No laughing matter. (woozily) but effi –
effing-caceous. Oh, Alas!
I lie, my racquet laid across my breast,
A fallen knight upon a stretcher-tomb,
at rest.

*lights down. mouth organ music indicating scene change hinting that
Alfie/God is influencing Laura's life*

*lights up on front cubicle curtain scene depicting the entrance into
operating theatre in large NHS hospital*

Laura wheeled in lying propped up on a gurney.

Surgeon   *(enters)* Still playing tennis at your age –
seventy-four! Bit risky, eh?

Laura I love the game and intend to play once more.
(beat) Operating at your age! Aren't you a little young? Bit risky, eh?

Surgeon Touché! Touché! I will see you tomorrow morning *(exits)*

Laura He smiles, his teeth agleam, and I go under, over, far away. Though rugger size he operates with delicate precision, screws in a plate.
(beat) I can relate no more for I have drifted off *(music)* away from the actual to the real – somewhere else – sorting – sifting meaning – me – us – why – what - heart – head – and something else – demanding, calling:
(calls out loudly) What's it all about, Alfie?

lights fade down mouth organ music indicating scene change.

a cubicle in a orthopaedic ward with front curtain drawn back.

lights fade up. Laura is lying on top of her bed with her leg in plaster.

Alfie is materialising through a puff of smoke he is sitting on her bed.

Alfie / God (From now on titled Alfie)
Well, well, well! What have we got here then? Hello, Peg leg! Here you are in this orthopaedic ward – not able to move much. A nice little gift all this *(indicating*

ward) from me to you, instead of flowers.

Laura   Some grievous, shitty gift! *(beat)* Alfie, it's incredible seeing you. How'd you get in here?

Alfie   Easy, Princess. You called me up – and asked me quite a question. Now I'll ask it you. What's it all about, love?

Laura   About the accident for starters. It's mucked my life up.

Alfie   Accident? Call it an accident?

Laura   It was outrageous. I am so pissed off and angry, and that I'm stuck in here. Just when I thought I'd got my life together. A nice balance of not too much work, sport, holidays, good home and money in the bank – cruising well toward my sunset. Then Crack! Stopped in my tracks.

Alfie   Quite so! Wrong track. A good thing too.

Laura   *(crossly)* Alfie!

Alfie   Your life of late has been do, do and do.

Laura   And now that's spoilt – I'm not able to do anything.
(childishly) It's just not fair!

Alfie	*(mock fatherly)* <u>There, there! There, there!</u> *(beat)* It's brought us two together Laura love.
Laura	Why me?
Alfie	You needed a break.
Laura	Oh, funny!
Alfie	From your full-up/rushing/sterile/materialistic/self-absorbed/unfulfilling – call it a life?
Laura	Come off it, Alfie! Stop lecturing me! *(self-righteously)* I do do a lot of gardening.
Alfie	However, so 'green' of you! But mostly you're a moaner. *(whiney voice)* 'This accident – I can't do anything.' Bodily that's so, but *(dramatically)* 'twas your soul that bade me hither. And thus I'm here!
Laura	I'm glad of that – so very glad of that. And glad too that these chintzy, jolly curtains are emboxing us, protecting us from those awful patients here. *(beat)* It's pretty intimate Alfie, just you and me.
Alfie	Just as it needs to be, Princess. *(puts arm around her)* After all you must be aware that I'm inside you.
Laura	*(false modestly)* Oh, Alf<u>eee</u>! At my age!

Alfie   Sacred congress – quite risqué, eh! *(both laugh)*

Laura Alfie   But seriousleee. *(they laugh)*

Alfie   You get yourself all worked up. You rage against what happened. So stroppy, love! It was no accident – it was a gift.

Laura   Another of your lovely gifts! Ta ever so!

Alfie   Trust me. *(beat)* Breaking your leg is no big deal. Not so your attitude – that's near to zero. You're on 'The Road <u>Most</u> Travelled'. Not becoming!

Laura   *(misinterpreting)* Becoming? *(self-pitying)* What can become of me? *(beat)* I'm pissed off too and angry with these people here. A damned cheek! An imposition! A public ward! A hellhole for healing!

Alfie goes to draw back the curtains

Laura   Don't Alfie! Oh, my God!

Alfie   *(bowing)* You called me, m'lady? *(imitating Laura's disdain, and accent)* 'These people here' *(normal voice)* are here to help you, and you them.

Laura   Listen to those cubicles of moaning, farting, throwing up, demented, blathering, 'bed-pan please' people.

Alfie   Never pee, Princess? Never been taken short?

Laura   *(almost ranting)* Have a look at those nurses, barely speaking English, missing veins, tight tourniquet-ing when mea-suring 'raised-by-them' blood pressure, nocturnal monsters, clanking, shouting, laughing – depriving me of sleep – of healing sleep – and Alfie, those cut-out men in suits who come each morning surrounded by their fawning entourage – indifferent and different each time. And sloppy Caribbean so-called cleaners flopping M.R.S.A and mops around, and the food purveyors......

Alfie   Hold on there! Hold on! Stop your whingeing Princess – these are the folk I love.

Laura   Bully for you, Alfie! *(beat)* For me – well *(starts to cry)* well......

Alfie   <u>A well is deep, my love. Look deep. Think deeply too.</u>

pause

Laura   *(in tears)* <u>Dear God! How I'd like to think and feel like you.</u>
To be inclusive, accepting, loving. Not

resisting, endlessly rejecting and conflict-
ing. Aloof I am and offish. Lonely. *(beat)*
I thought it was my leg was broken – not
me.
(beat) <u>Alfie, Oh Alfie, what to do?</u>

Alfie   <u>You're lucky, Princess – an opportunity</u>
<u>is handed you.</u> Ten days at least to start
to work things out. You've dramatis
personae captured in those beds – and
many walk on parts. *(dramatically)* All
the ward's your stage. *(beat)* And I will
be around to help. *(beat)* Cheer up love,
here's a tissue. *(Laura blows her nose) (cheer-
fully)* Let's play a game.
A conundrum. What's the highest,
lowest, widest, top-of-the-pops feeling
that could make the world go round and
round – a happier place?

Laura   Er…er…Sex?

Alfie   Nope.

Laura   Lerve?

Alfie   Nope. You're getting warmer. Not sex,
not love, but close to love.

Laura   Um…um…give me a clue.

Alfie   A C word, Princess. It begins with C.

pause

Alfie   Com…

Laura   Com?…

Both   passion.

Laura   Compassion

Alfie   Right, you've got it right. How to com-
               pash is lesson number one.

Laura   How will that help?

Alfie   Trust me, darling. *(jokingly eerie)* Woo-
               hoo! Mysterious ways! *(beat)* Ta ra – got
               to leave you now. I've got a mission. You
               need a kip. Over to you, Princess – love
               yer. Ta ra!

Alfie adjusts the side curtains lights dimmed.

Laura   *(big sigh)* Love you too, Alfie. *(mouth organ
               dreamtime music)* For you, for me, for you
               who's me, I'll try to 'do' compassion.
               (yawning, going to sleep) I'll take some notes
               – maybe a short story or a script for a
               film. I'll take some of these creatures in
               the ward as my principal characters – see
               if before Laura, that's me, leaves hospital
               she can tolerate them – maybe even care
               for them – and *(singing)* 'wiv a little bit of
               luck' *(speaking)* like Alfie, love them.

Alfie   *(speaks from off stage until he returns)* Put in

some of the supporting cast too – nurses,
suits, doctors,…

Laura   *(sleepily)* Wankers!

Alfie   Food…

Laura   Ugh! Awful!

Alfie   Food-trolley ladies. And those cleaners.

Laura   *(disparagingly)* Disease is snarling in those
mops. Bit part players.
OK Alfie. *(beat)* You said you weren't
stopping.

Alfie   A habit of mine – constant eavesdrop-
ping.
(beat) Bo-peep now, Princess.

Laura   Good on you, Alfie. *(beat)* It's so outrageous that my body's hurt, when already
at my age it's falling apart – and there I
was trying to stay fit, well fit-ish, playing
tennis. Look where that got me! *(beat)*
Glad though that my soul didn't forget
the soul bit.
You know Alfie… *(beat)* Alfie are you
there?

Alfie   I'm listening.

Laura   That accident was out of all proportion
to that little volleying jump – Crack!

Crack! Twist! Inconceivable! It seemed
from out of space, as if my bones cracked
in mid-air. I hardly touched the ground
– but it felled me. *(beat)* OK Alfie, no
accident – a timely intervention.

dreamland music off.

lights up as Alfie arrives in puff of smoke

Alfie   I'm back. Mission completed. *(beat)*
Timely? I've mentioned to you before
how I consider time – there is none.
None except now. Now or never!
(claps loudly)

Laura   *(startled)* Alfie, don't do that – I'm still
half asleep.

Alfie   You're telling me!

Laura   You're waking me up!

Alfie   That's what it's all about. Waking you up
is my intention. *(beat)* There's only the
present, Princess. Past and future are not
actual.

Laura   Don't give me concepts I can't get my
head around.

Alfie   You've already got your head round it –
thought it, otherwise how could I have
said it?

Laura I'm not following you.

Alfie Wake up! Let's get this act together. *(beat)* There's a lot more going on than you're aware of. *(briskly)* Now then, lesson number one. Non-existing time may be running in or out. Maybe you have ten days, or thirty minutes depending on the length of the programme left to be recorded – all is recorded, don't you know?

Laura Recorded? *(suspiciously)* You know something I don't?

Alfie So it would seem. *(beat)* You're writing your own story. Ain't that so Princess?

Laura So to speak? Or really? *(bewildered)* Hey, Ho! Hey, Ho! *(beat)* Where to start?

Alfie You've this lady on your left. Tell me about her.

lights slightly up in adjacent cubicle. just the suggestion of Doreen's form propped up in bed

Laura *(petulant)* Some Lady! She's tiresome. I've tried to block her out – so many visitors, endlessly chattering – even taking my chair. *(beat)* Her full name's Doreen, Doreen Black. She's very, very old, and very lame. They had to re-operate as her hip came out all crooked.

Alfie goes over to Doreen and plumps up her pillows.

Laura speaks to herself; she is disgusted by Doreen and hopes Alfie can't hear

Laura   <u>She's like an injured moulting bird,</u>
<u>The time and effort spent on her is quite</u>
<u>absurd.</u>
<u>Her scrawny arms are bruised black blue</u>
<u>and yellow.</u>
<u>Decaying, unsavoury – a near cadaver.</u>
(to Alfie who has returned) I've already
learnt that she had eight kids, six still
alive – twelve grandchildren and eighteen great-grandchildren. Have you
noticed Alfie that it is the wrong people
who over populate?

Alfie   *(incredulously)* Is that so? *(beat)* I sometimes think the world would be a better
place full of folk like the Blacks.

Laura   Don't be daft! She can't even get the
nurse on time – doesn't seem to know
how to work, or can't be fussed to use
the call button.

Doreen   Quick, nurse, it's coming. Quick!

Laura   Not raising her voice loud enough for
them to hear. Then the inevitable accident.

Nurse 1   *(Enters. Stands beside Doreen. No other move-*

174

ment.) Not to worry, Doris dear, we need to put you in your chair. Shall we move our behind a little up the bed?

Laura For heaven's sake, it's not the nurse's arse is it? And why doesn't Doreen get organised – speak louder or learn to use......

Alfie That nurse is better at empathy than you.

Laura Empathy?

Alfie To be in someone else's shoes. Compassion's cousin – lesson number two.

Nurse 1 Come on Doreen, let's have a practice. They're not all that easy to work, these call machines. Let me show you.

Laura Compassion, empathy – you're overworking me.

Alfie Vitamins for your soul. *(beat)* I commend that nurse's choice of words. She said 'behind'. Bottom's too childish, and arse – your word – too crude for someone like Doreen – the nurse didn't tick her off – she was more sensitive than you! *(nurse exits)* She might be a foreigner but she's more skilled with words than you. Call yourself a writer! (beat) And by the way love, you're no Spring chicken. *(quoting)* 'Not moulting as yet, but an injured bird.'

Laura Alfie, you snoop. I hoped you had not heard.
(beat) This is the most difficult time in my life, worse than my teens – I hate getting old – sagging flesh – forgetfulness – needing your glasses to find your glasses – hearing aids – sensible shoes – I hate old age.

Tone and Charmian enter Doreen's cubicle

Alfie And seemingly yourself. *(beat)* I hold dear old people. All they have lived and learnt. I like tracing their wrinkles.

Laura Botox to you! *(beat)* Listen, Alfie. Two of her children – well, middle-aged children – are with her now.

Alfie I'm all ears, Princess.

Tone We'll have you out of here in no time.

Doreen *(weakly)* No, Tone, I'll be home no more. I'll not get to walk again.

Tone Come on Mum! We need you. We miss your Sunday dinner.

Charmian Melanie knitted this pink bed-jacket for you – not bad for a twelve year old! I think her homework suffered. Here, let's try it on.

Tone   That looks nice, Mum. And Frank's spent his pocket money on some After Eights for you. Soft, he said; no need to put in your teeth.

Doreen   Cheeky, tell him he's a cheeky monkey.

Tone   That's better. Nice to see a smile. By the way, baby Babs will be one this week, Jan'll bring her to you. She's ever so bonny – looks just like you about the eyes.

Doreen   Denis – how's Denis?

Charmian   Leeds's a long way off, but he sends his love and is fixing to come. 'Charm,' he said to me, 'tell Nan not to give up. Tell her to lie back and think of England!'

Doreen   Think of England – don't think I want to. Down the drain. Not like…

Tone, Charmian
            (imitating Doreen, but kindly) 'Not like when I was young.'

Doreen giggles

Tone   Some of the others will visit tomorrow.

Charmian   Yes – Terry, Joan, Ruthie, Martin and Pip, who wanted to bring her baby rabbit – Flopsie.

Laura   *(mockingly)* Uncle Tom Cobleigh and all!

Tone   Time's up Mum, I can hear the food trolley. *(beat)* Charm, got Mum's laundry?

Charmian   Yep. Bye for now, Mum – <u>we've tired you out with all our talking.</u>

Tone   *(encouragingly)* <u>You've got the physios tomorrow to start you on walking.</u> *(turning to Laura)* You've dropped your magazine, my dear. *(picks up glossy magazine and hands it to Laura)* There you are!

Laura   *(disconcerted)* Oh, oh…thank you…you shouldn't have troubled…

Tone   No trouble, a pleasure. We were wondering if you could keep an eye on Mum, she's a bit low. *(pause)* My name is Tone.

Laura   *(reticently)* And mine is Laura.

Charmian   We'll be visiting again in the next few days. Want us to bring you anything?

Laura   *(confused, embarrassed)* No, no, really not – thank you though – thanks.

they leave saying goodbye and words of encouragement to Doreen

and Laura. *'Behave yourselves' 'No midnight feasts' 'Take care'*
'Bye now' etc.

Laura   She's left alone now propped up against
her pillows, waiting for her dinner. She's
taking her teeth out of a paper cup and
is putting them in. *(pause)* Now popping
seedless grapes into her mouth and at
the same time smiling in the warmth of
her family's in-articulated love. *(pause)*
And now the After Eights. *(beat)* My
hunch is, Alfie, that Doreen might make
it.

Alfie   *(agreeing)* Mm-mm. Mm-mm. You might
be right there.

Doreen   Here, have one love. If you can reach
them.

Alfie   Go on, Princess! *(pause)* Show a leg!

Laura   Not funny, Alfie. (beat) I'll get my walker.
Hateful hints of Zimmer life to come.

(moves to Doreen's bedside, still in half light.)

Laura   Hello Doreen, my name is Laura.

Doreen   Hello, Laura love.

Laura   *(hesitantly)* Well, er, hello, yes, thank you
– yes I'd like one. You know After Eights
are my favourites too.

Alfie   *(whispers, pleased with himself)* Well, well, well. What a coincidence!

The sound of paper being torn off and the box being passed between them as they sit eating away – the occasional 'Here, dear' 'Thanks' 'Have another' 'Really shouldn't' etc. Mouth organ music indicating scene change starts in the background, then takes over. Lights fade to black in both cubicles. Alfie exits. Lights upon Laura.

Laura   *(writing in her notebook)* Wednesday after lunch Zimmered over to Doreen. Exchanged news of our families – my two children living abroad, and hers mostly local. Except the one in Leeds *(looks up from writing)* must remember his name. Asked her about her famous Sunday lunches. *(light slightly up in Doreen's cubicle)*

Doreen   *(Laura takes notes as Doreen speaks)* Roast meat, roast spuds and veg. And loads of gravy. Then pudding: pie, often apple for the grown-ups and something special for the children.

Laura   *(taking notes)* The ATS in the war. Fell in love with Ray, a corporal – died twelve years ago.

Doreen   He'd had a real tough life, worn out at seventy-four. You know something Laura, we were lovebirds 'til the day he died. *(lights fade)*

Laura	Lovebirds! D's story's grabbing me; maybe I could base a character on her. Just remembered – Denis from Leeds is her son's name……

Alfie enters in puff of smoke and clears his throat to get Laura's attention

Laura	Alfie! Alfie, are you really here? Or are you a morphine incarnation? Am I just imagining you?
Alfie	<u>I'm here! And all those other times – because you needed me.</u>
Laura	<u>And if I hadn't needed you, you mean to say you wouldn't be?</u> Are you suggesting I created you to fit my need? Alfie, are you not you in your own right?
Alfie	Never asked myself that question – seems irrelevant. <u>You know my love, many people say</u> *(theatrically)* <u>'Twas I created them. Don't pother your pretty head in such a way. You might puzzle me completely out of existence! As I'm here dear Princess can I be of assistance?</u>
Laura	You can. *(beat)* By the way your last couplet was disastrous!
Alfie	Maybe you should write some proper

poetry – not all this dodgy doggerel.

Laura   Yes. *(beat)* I need your assistance. Something happened this morning on the
ward round. It made me feel, well,
almost panicky. As usual the sycophantic
entourage. Exhausted nurses waiting
for release, and new doctors who don't
know me and I don't know them. Let's
hope they confer with one another from
time to time. And one of them was
really dishy – seriously so. Too young for
me. *(beat)* More accurately, and boo-hoo
sadly, me too old for him. But seriouslee
attractive. I lusted for him Alfie – Oops!
to put it a little more delicately, and
inaccurately – I really fancied him. *(beat)*
And this is where I need your help. It's
this business of old age,my old age, and
how it depresses me. Most people in this
ward are geriatrics and are starting to
infect me. This leg in plaster doesn't help
– and that hateful walking frame. Alfie,
I just don't 'do' Old Age. *(beat)* Before
that fatal tennis game I felt, well, not old
– elderly at a pinch. I felt attractive – a
sexy septuagenarian. 'Sacred' congress Alfie, is not enough for me. That
toothsome doctor looked at me as if I
weren't there – a lump of flesh that he
or someone else had cut into. I felt as if I
were on a conveyor belt and had arrived
at the place where labels were stuck on

me. 'Old.' 'Not desirable.' 'Shelf life over.' 'Not fit for purpose.' *(beat)* It's not as if when Michael and I make love we ever think of sagging breasts, fat stomachs, baldness, aches and pains. All those deterioration things seemed, your wordAlfie, irrelevant. But that was then. Michael desired me and me him – then! But now I feel humiliated, seen for what I look like. I no longer desire myself, my life, and think no-one could want me, let alone touch me. I feel revolting. Old and revolting. Decrepitude. *(beat)* Sorry Alfie, not very spiritual – let's say corporeal.

Alfie   Bodies can be a problem! How they wax and wane. 'Ebb and flow by the moon.' *(beat)* Feel better now you've sounded off? Got it off your sagging chest? *(beat)* Princess, find a place beyond complaint and rage.

Laura   *(incredulous)* Hah?

Alfie   There is one. I testify! Compash and laughter might help you start to 'do' Old Age. *(beat)* Why put bad images into the air? Why give them substance? Words are powerful as you ought to know!

Laura   I feel degraded.

Alfie   Only   because   you   grade   yourself   by

other people's values.

Laura   We're getting oh-so profoundly serious. You know Alfie most people that I know switch off when they hear this sort of stuff. Prefer light entertainment – a giggle a minute. That's why I think my writing isn't marketable – too fucking serious. Laura's a borer!

Alfie   In my immodest opinion Princess, not exactly a borer, but heav<u>eee</u>, a gloom-er-doomer. Un-colourful, not authentic, too edited – you've rated yourself along-side other writers and got lost. Lighten up, Princess. You've lost your ability to dance.

Laura   One legged, ancient ballerina!

Alfie   *(enthusiastically)* Original! A syncopated crutch-dance! *(beat)* Earnest sometimes you are, not serious! *(beat)* I get a stom-ach ache when I hear canned laughter. Let the giggles-a-minuters switch off, it really doesn't matter. Let them live their giggly way. *(beat)* You need a new language Princess, in your being and in your writing.

Laura   Meaning?

Alfie   You could do with a bit of that too. *(beat)*

If you could change the way you feel – about being old – you could help a bit towards altering the way other people see old age. All this gerontophobia!

Laura   Ugly word for an ugly prejudice.

Alfie   And one that you don't have? *(beat)* Change your vocabulary, brighten up your images. Get them into your writing, into your speaking.

Laura   Example, Alfie.

Alfie   Example, Laura. These folk in here are not *(quoting)* 'in the winter of their lives' *(pause. pleased with himself)* it is their 'time of harvest'. How's that?

Laura   Pretty good! A little churchy.

Alfie   A positive new image of ageing.

Laura   You'd better write the poems!

Alfie   Enough talk! Let's introduce some action. But before we do we've three themes to chew over. Number one: compassion. That takes in empathy and is in the script already; but they need to be throughout. Two: laughter. Not nearly enough for my liking, but starting to be introduced. Theme Three: a new language, not doggerel but poetry. *(after-thought)* And dancing on one leg.

Laura   That's four, not three – you're getting carried away! *(beat)* I like the menu, Alfie.

Alfie   Pleased to pleasure you, Princess. I'll now serve it up. Here goes. Theme Three needs working on, and sorting out. *(beat)* And so – how about telling me about Catherine, in the bed on your right? *(Catherine's cubicle lights up slightly. Catherine's form is seen sitting on her bed)*

Laura   *(severely)* I've asked to have her moved, or at least sedated. Why can't the Alzhei-mers have a ward of their own? *(beat)* She slipped and had a bad fall at her ninetieth birthday party – imagine celebrating at such an age and in such a senile state – how unseemly – what's the point?

Alfie   It was a great do! I was as pleased as punch to be there. Catherine is very rich, so Veuve Cliquot flowed, and we all had a happy time. She even sang a caba-ret song – she was famous you know. She held the tune, with a little bit of help from my harmonica, but invented new words. I liked it better than the original.

Laura   Words, words! How she gabbles on.

Catherine Yoo-hoo! Yoo-hoo! Help me! Help me!

Alfie	Why don't you Laura?
Laura	Help <u>me</u> to have some quiet!
Catherine	Coo-ee! Coo-ee! Some-one…two… three, come here! *(phrases in bold show when Catherine is trying to get through to Laura)* **I don't know, do you? I flow, do you?** *(as if hurt)* Don't <u>do</u> that – what are you <u>doing</u>? *(beat)* **Always do, do, do.**
Laura	*(startled)* What's that? Hear that Alfie? Didn't you say that to me just a little while ago? What's going on?
Alfie	*(echo-y repeat of when he first said it)* Your life of late has been do, do, and do.
Catherine	Is anybody hearing me?
Laura	I can't but hear you. You go on and on. *(beat)* <u>Last night she managed to get out of her barred bed, and wandered nearly falling, nearly falling on my bed and leg.</u>
Alfie	Dog-ger-<u>rel</u>!
Laura	I pushed the <u>bell</u>. <u>'Nurse, I need to sleep, can't you sedate her?'</u>
Nurse 2	*(enters Catherine's cubicle)* <u>No opiate for patients with dementia.</u>
Laura	*(despairingly)* Me, then.

Nurse 2   Now then Catherine me darling back to
                   bed with you.

*Catherine has a beautiful singing voice she starts to sing happy
sounding gibberish to tune of 'When Irish Eyes are Smiling'. nurse
exits. When Alfie joins in accompanying her on his mouth organ she
finds some of the words from the lyric.*

*She has a beautiful singing voice she starts to sing happy sounding
gibberish to tune of 'When Irish Eyes are Smiling'. Nurse exits.
When Alfie joins in accompanying her on his mouth organ she finds
some of the words from the lyric.*

Catherine   When Irish eyes are smiling,
                  Sure, 'tis like the morn in Spring,
                  In the lilt of Irish laughter
                  You can hear the angels sing.
                  When Irish hearts are happy,
                  All the world seems bright and gay.
                  And when Irish eyes are smiling,
                  Sure, they steal your heart away.

They finish a verse with a flourish, and clap.

Laura   I am starting to hate her and the noisy
                  nonsense that so upsets me.

Alfie   Lighten up, love! You listen to Cath-
                  erine, but haven't heard a word she's
                  spoken. In spite of yourself some of
                  what she said has got to you.

Laura   Nonsense. Nonsense. It's all nonsense.

Alfie	Listen to her, Laura. Start to understand her.
Laura	Gibberish! Balderdash!
Alfie	Better than Beckett – and she's here in real life, and been given you.
Laura	Another of your grotty gifts – thank you so much! For God's sake, here she goes again.
Catherine	Yoo-hoo you! Yoo-hoo! **Who is that there, who are you, who?**
Alfie	Hear that Princess? Hear that? You need to find out. *(pause)* Cat got your tongue?
Laura	*(apprehensively)* Laura. My name is Laura.
Catherine	Laura...bore(r)...alis. No warmth. Cold. Snow. *(describing the Northern Lights very poetically)* Dark/night/glow/curtain. Red/green/blue/purple whirls of light wisping. Swir *(elongate)* rl. *(Catherine imitates the Nanny she had when she was a child)* Kate, do not wave or stare or they will swoop down and grab you! *(as if to one of the hospital nurses)* Don't you touch me like that – leave the nightlight on! *(child-like)* Katie's scared in the dark.

To give herself courage she la-las the tune of 'You'll Never Walk Alone', putting some random words into it, including 'dark' 'don't be afraid'.

Catherine   Yoo-hoo! You two! Yoo-hoo! *(la-las tune. Invites them to join in)* You too. *(hooting realistically)* Twit-twoo!

Alfie   Come on Laura – give it a go. I'll play along with you – keep you in tune!

Alfie plays the tune on his mouth organ. Laura and Catherine sing together, la-la-ing, and introducing some words from the song. From time to time Laura sings lines from the lyric.

Laura   When you walk through a storm
Hold you head up high
And don't be afraid of the dark.
At the end of the storm is a golden sky
And the sweet silver song of the lark.
Walk on through the wind,
Walk on through the rain,
Tho' your dreams be tossed and blown.
Walk on, walk on with hope in your
heart
And you'll never walk alone,
You'll never, ever walk alone
Walk on, walk on with hope in your
heart
And you'll never walk alone,
You'll never, ever walk alone.

It ends with both singing the line 'Don't be afraid of the dark'. All three laugh warmly.

Lights fade down Change of scene music Lights up on Laura.

Laura   *(on telephone)* Thank you for phoning
             back Michael. I was feeling really bad.
             (pause) I was so cold on your visit. *(pause)*
             But something is lifting. Like I'm thaw-
             ing. *(pause)* Yes, I do too. I'll be your
             one-legged lovebird......

Alfie   *enters in puff of smoke, theatrically clears his
             throat*

Laura   *(whispers to Alfie)* Hi, Alfie. How was that
             Alfie?

Alfie   Sounds promising.

Laura   *(on telephone)* I must ring off. My therapist
             has just arrived. Goodbye darling, good-
             bye for now. *(rings off)* Good to see you,
             Alfie.

Alfie   And how can 'your therapist' help you?

Laura   You already have – introducing me
             to Catherine and her gobbledegook.
             I loved her 'Lauraborealis', and her
             colourful use of words. I'd give anything
             to be able to write like that; albeit, a little
             more coherently.

Alfie   Poetry instead of doggerel. Perhaps

she'll infect you! *(beat)* I love to listen to
Catherine singing.

Laura   What a voice! We had a bit of a sing-
song at tea time – the trolley lady joined
in – we ended up with a calypso, she
swinging her hips and dancing with the
tea-pot. She made us laugh. The head
nurse came along and shushed us up!

Alfie   Now <u>you're</u> getting carried away! Your
imagination is running away with you!
You think anyone would credit that happening in real life?

Laura   Poetic licence!

Alfie   Other cast members been around?

Laura   Yes, yesterday…could you hand me
that exercise book – behind the water
bottle – thanks. I'm keeping a sort of
notebook/journal. *(reading)* Tuesday.
Just notes Alfie. Cleaners – still slopping
super-bugs around, but one of them
seemed to take more care after we got
into a bit of a conversation – she's West
Indian and has two young kids back
home being looked after by her mother
– her husband walked out on her. I don't
know what she lives on as she sends
at least half of her paltry pay back to
them. As I know you like to know people

by their names, I jotted down her kids'.
'Precious' for the girl and 'Cosmos' for
her son. How about that!

Alfie   They miss each other something awful.
(beat) But at least the kids are with their
Gran and are being brought up in the
sun. Precious, Cosmos – great names –
have a ring to them.

Laura   That's what I almost thought but stopped
myself. More fun and special than Jane/
Jim/John, or Alfie for that matter. She's
going to bring a snapshot of them next
time she cleans in here. I don't think
I'd have survived being parted from my
kids like that – and this awful English
weather. *(beat)* I remember in the old days
fierce starched Matron took interest in
the wards being cleaned – now there is
no-one. I don't think those cleaners feel
part of the scene, or feel that they play
any part at all in our well-being.

Alfie   Even you called them bit part players.

Laura   *(ignoring his comment)* Just a commercial
arrangement and unfair minimum
wages. And now C Difficile – better to
say than to have – to add to their worries.

Alfie   Other dramatis personae? *(moves back-
stage)*

Laura	*(reading from her notebook)* Wednesday ward round. No disparaging ageist dishy doctor, but my rugger playing surgeon. *(surgeon enters)* <u>Once more he smiled with warmth (and I smiled back!) his teeth agleam.</u>
Surgeon	<u>You're doing well. No medication, no morphine.</u>
Laura	So Alfie, you can't just be a morphine hallucination.
Surgeon	<u>We've nicknamed you Navratilova.</u>
Laura	<u>You mean like her my tennis isn't over?</u>
Surgeon	We did a good job. Throughout the operation we had it in mind that *(gently teasing her)* you need to be fit for Wimbledon next year. You'll have to do a lot of re-hab: work.
Laura	I will, I will. *(beat)* Forgive me, I'm really sorry but I don't recall your name.
Surgeon	Mr Marshall. James Marshall.
Laura	Mr James Marshall.
Surgeon	Learn to use your crutches whilst you are here – you've the physios each day, so take advantage of their help.

Laura I will, I will. *(beat)* Thank you Mr Marshall for my successful op: *(beat)* I'll do my best with the crutches – I really hate that Zimmerframe. They could at least be painted in bright colours.

Surgeon I'll suggest it to Maintenance! *(beat)* And thank you, Navratilova. Thank you Laura. *(beat)* I'll see you once again on your discharge. Goodbye for now. *(exits)*

Alfie moves back to Laura

Laura What do you think of that Alfie? Eh? Thanking me for what?

Alfie Perhaps for seeing a different point of view. Meeting you has helped him look at old people a little differently.

Laura He seemed to have forgotten I was seventy-four, and you know…

Alfie Yes!

Laura Those medics did confer together even if only about that old gal playing tennis…

Alfie Yes, I heard them. But my love, they did not talk like you thought. It was a serious conversation – and they called you by your proper name.

Laura   And he used it when he came to see me. *(pleased)* He knew my name.

Alfie   *(slightly admonishing)* Yet you hadn't bothered to remember his! He was just that 'not private/second rate/NHS (Ugh!) surgeon' to you. Not young James Marshall with a life, and with a skill and great gift as a surgeon. You're pretty ugly-ly egocentric, Princess. Love and interest need go both ways. Two to tango, don't yer know. Your self-absorption keeps you mean and lonely.

Laura   You don't half not pull your punches Alfie. *(beat)* At least I thanked him.

Alfie   And you meant it. *(beat)* So, you are beginning to 'do' gratitude! You get a brownie point for that.

Laura   Ta ever so!

Alfie   You've already some for compash, and one or two just lately for laughter.

Laura   Great!

Alfie   You're getting there. So how about number three?

Laura   Number three?

Alfie   Language. You mentioned en passant

that Catherine had inspired you.

Laura   I'm self conscious about reading you my poems.

Alfie   Poemzzz! How many have you written? *(beat)* Well, let's start with just one!

Laura   I'll find them. *(pause)* Back of the note-book – upside down.

Alfie   That's a good start.
(beat) 'You're old Mother Laura the young doctor said,
and you hair has become very white,
and yet you're beginning to stand on your head,
do you think at your age it is right?'
(Laura laughs delightedly)
Changing the subject, and moving on apace – how do you feel about Catherine?

Laura   She troubles me less – in fact I now quite like her company. Her language and singing cheers me up – started me off on a poem – she's deliciously irreverent.

Alfie   And how does Catherine look?

Laura   What do you mean?

Alfie   Cor-por-really!

Laura   She looks…Oh, I don't know – <u>alluring
               and intriguing; she fascinates me for
               what she is revealing</u> – some lovely qual-
               ity from deep inside.

Alfie   I meant, what thinkest thou of her
               ninety year old dilapidation?

Laura   I haven't noticed. I've noticed other
               things. *(reprimanding)* Alfie you shouldn't
               speak of her like that.

Alfie   Proving a point, m'lady! *(beat)* Let's hear
               that poem.

Laura   Not sure of a title yet. Provisionally
               called Catherine. 'I trace your lines…'

Alfie   Sounds familiar. I think I've heard that
               somewhere before!

Laura   '…your life imprinted on that wrinkled
               crinkled tissue face.
               I'm glad you did not Botox them away.
               I can imagine how that smile lit up
               those whom you loved, and who loved
               you.
               Your lovely laugh lines.
               Frown creases indicate your questioning,
               your puzzling at life's vagaries.
               Those wavy furrows deep across your
               brow
               tell me how you wonder-worshipped
               watching whirling colours in the sky.

Wrinkles do not lie.
The expression of your singing etched,
around your well kissed lips.
The lyrical, the dark, the passionate, the
funny.
No photograph or painting could por-
tray
the magic you possess the way your face
does.
And how you can become the owl that
hoots.'
pause
Well, what do you think?

Alfie   Good. Good. Especially the last line.
(beat) Now then, give us another. Just
one, mind you. Choose well because I
want to set it to music so that we can
finish off with a bang!

Laura   OK. OK. As you know Alfie I don't sing
that well.

Alfie   You didn't do too badly with Catherine.
You could always speak it with the music
in the background.

Laura   I haven't thought what to call it yet, so
I'll just start right in.
'We'll pack up a picnic and go down to
the bay,
I'll put food in a haversack
So your hands will be free for me.
In the sea's tide, let there be

breakers for cross-currents,
not for the surge.
'Let us walk slowly,
aware of great movement in our small
steps,
aware of great love in small gestures,
and enjoy ourselves on the way.' *(pause)*
Well, what do you think?

Alfie   Good. Good. Especially the last line.
(beat) I may not use all of the poem –
maybe just the last verse. Do you mind?

Laura   That's OK by me.

Alfie   I'll see. Just a minute *(arty voice)* while I
do my composing. *(hums a bit of the tune
and dances around)* There!

Pause

Alfie   Well folks, thanks for listening to Laura's story and *(singing)* wiv a little bit of
luck *(speaking)* <u>hearing!</u> *(beat)* She was
unaware that her 'Break a Leg' tale was
being recorded – though I did mention it to her. I am you know, a bit of
a manipulative magician! And here's
another conundrum for you: has this
bit of Laura's life taken 45 minutes, ten
days – or longer/shorter? Proving, as is
my wont, that definitive time does not
exist – not to labour the point! <u>And what</u>

is what – and who is who? And who said what? Us, me or you?

Laura Alfie   Dumpty-Dum Dumpty-Dum Dumpty-Dum.

Alfie   Was it just chatter? And does it matter?

Laura   Everything matters.

Pause

Alfie   And doesn't matter.

Pause

Alfie   *(aside)* So – Be – It. *(beat)* To end or begin with, Laura and I would like to entertain you by giving you the piece we've just composed – hers the lyric and mine the tune. You've already heard the words.

Laura   Good thing too. I'm not sure you'll hear them when I'm singing! It's called 'Love'.

Alfie   Here goes. *(plays a little stops to audience)* Enjoy! Love yer!

Laura speaks the first two verses over the music. She sings the last

Laura   'We'll pack up a picnic and go down to the bay,
I'll put food in a haversack

So your hands will be free for me.
In the sea's tide let there be
breakers for cross-currents,
not for the surge.
Let us walk slowly,
aware of great movement in our small
steps,
aware of great love in small gestures,
and enjoy ourselves on the way.'

the sound of the mouth organ fades as do the lights

THE END

I had left The Hut door open and have gone back in.

Chapter Twenty-Eight
The Hut
Willow Cabin

Now back to the Beeootiful Game how important it was
to me from the age of eight I played tennis albeit sort of
pat ball in Devon we had a court Gill and I had a come-
back a tennis ball on an elastic a big frame so it was at the
same height as when the ball comes at you over the net
hour after hour I would hit that ball at school I had coaching with Mr Brewer too old to go to the war I enjoyed
the shape of the shots the rhythm and the follow through
the almost dance position of the feet I liked the strategy
the cunning in placing the ball the energising feeling of
intending to win the way the classically executed shots
worked best but what I loved most was getting into the
flow way back when I was about twelve it was sports day
and it was the first time I experienced it an inter house
relay race and I am passed the baton I fly although my
feet are on the ground I just let myself run and nothing
else time does not exist except it did as my run was timed
and it was a record reflecting afterwards I felt I had got
from A to B in one movement with no physical effort at
all lying here on the hut's comfortable bed I can relive
that magical event preciselyI know I was completely in the
moment a pinnacle moment I wasn't surprised or proud
of my record it was just naturally so even at that age I

became desirous of being in the flow the zone as often as I could although I couldn't put it into words then almost can't now my body and mind in one there you are it is intrinsically rewarding addictive so back to tennis when I was totally focused loose relaxed somehow fluid in love with the game no worry or concern about winning or playing well or fear of losing when my skill was as honed as could be it happened just a sort of bliss then I was a good tennis player almost on a higher plane I wondered if I could train myself to be a zoner in many other spheres to a certain extent I have managed to do so meditation trains me helps me to cut out all that is extraneous and to consciously stay in the moment I would like to live all my life in this flow I am getting better at it spending time in that magical state when writing sometimes when writing poetry often dancing on my own all over the place at one with the music painting making love and now croquet it too is a beeootiful game most alice in wonderlandish the players are pretty old some a little like the red queen eccentric as many men as women I expect the balls to turn into hedgehogs and the mallets into flamingos at any time but as alice said in conclusion a very difficult game indeed it is a great game needing strategy and focus and a dead-eye which I have so once again if I can get into the zone I play well I must have no distraction which is difficult with so many singular characters around and the thought that often comes into my head that some of them might expire at any moment must be completely absorbed in the game free and loose but adhering to the skills keep your head down when you strike the ball in the flow state the ball sails through the hoop knocks the opponent's ball off the lawn with no strain at all curiouser and curiouser not quite explicable…

I am more often in the flow state now so flowing get out of bed the bedclothes tidy themselves up and I return from this real world to another.

Chapter Twenty-Nine
Houseboat

I am now over seventy. I have found what I was looking for. I had thought it imperative that my life have meaning, and have found that that meaning is being. In fact the questioning of meaning in life is not edifying, as someone, I can't remember who, said. I have an acknowledgement and a clearer understanding of God, and of quite a lot of other things.

As God's thoughts will no longer come in italics after I have finished writing this story I will listen and look. I am aware of the many ways that God is transmitted. I have decided to drop the God word. I find the naming somehow negating and diminishing. I know, but the way of knowing is incommunicable. It is as if I've got an inner sense that knows and connects me.

enough writing and reflection sarah there are many things to do

First of all I am getting in touch with John. In fact I already have, and it is on the cards that we might get together again. I never would have thought it!

i am a neat dealer

I am going to get involved in prison reform. I stated in the chapter about High Security Prisons what I think is necessary. Some good pressure groups already exist. As I can't do everything I will concentrate on helping the men when they are through their sentences. As I haven't as much energy as I had even when I was middle-aged, I intend to become the teacher. I will give myself the job of training people to do this work. They will learn to work alongside probation officers, and others who are, or should be, responsible for finding them housing. They will help the men applying for work, assist them in writing and applying for jobs, and rehearse them in how to present themselves in an interview, especially how to deal with the impediment they have with the disclosure of their criminal record. If I think some counselling is needed I or some colleagues will supply it.

I will create a charity and I am confidant (fairly) that the funding will be forthcoming.

I am not sure how to address this next one, but I'm looking into it. The law should be changed and many sexual offences should be re-classified, they are not crimes, they are illnesses. Recollecting and writing about my time in prisons and the therapeutic work I did there has made me aware that I am in a good position to be listened to.

Not sure yet who to get in touch with. I'll have to ask around.

As I can no longer play tennis I play a lot more croquet. I really enjoy it, and am pretty good! It gives me the opportunity to practise getting in the flow.

I now accept that I am not a very social being and will no longer chide myself for it. I often like to be on my own. It gives me time to listen. I never feel lonely or alone.

because you aren't

I realise that I have not seen enough of Timmy, Richard and Caroline and their families. By writing this autobiography I have freed myself, been freed of, all that bad mothering stuff. I think we would find our lives enriched by each other's company and have a lot of fun.

I have gone back to The Studio. I will start painting again quite soon.

We intend to train ourselves to use the gifts that we have.

I have learnt so much by telling you my story. I feel cleared. The ghosts are laid.

I now know better how to conduct my therapeutic work.

I am more often in the flow, sometimes when doing the most mundane of tasks.

And then there is all that writing, and John, my children, grandchildren, painting, reading, music, food, wine, and my new sport croquet!

Lightning Source UK Ltd.
Milton Keynes UK
UKOW04f1906220515

252154UK00004B/124/P

9 781909 477957